Eliza Merry is an arts and literature lecturer and a writer of prose and poetry. Her first book, *Thoughts of the Muses*, was published in 2022. She has also been commissioned over some years to write articles for literary and arts magazines. Eliza lives in Dorset in a five hundred year old cottage. Her fascination with the past and its untold stories, means the atmosphere of her ancient home creates a powerful stimulant to her historical imaginings. She also loves countryside walks, listening to music and opera, enjoying good food and spending time with family and friends.

To Arwen
with best wishes
from Eliza

The Lost Children of Fulhurst

Eliza Merry

The Lost Children of Fulhurst

Vanguard Press

A CIP catalogue record for this title is
available from the British Library.

ISBN 978 1 83794 042 4

*Vanguard Press is an imprint of
Pegasus Elliot Mackenzie Publishers Ltd.*
www.pegasuspublishers.com

This is a work of fiction. Names, characters, businesses, places, events and
incidents are either the product of the author's imagination or used in a
fictitious manner. Any resemblance to actual persons, living or dead, or actual
events is purely coincidental.

First Published in 2023

**Vanguard Press
Sheraton House Castle Park
Cambridge England**

Printed & Bound in Great Britain

This book is dedicated to: Ferdy, Gil, Magnus, Otto, Isla, Clara and Adelaide.

Apart from the county of Sussex and the towns of
Lewes, Crawley, Brighton and Eastbourne all locations in
this book are imaginary.
Likewise, all active characters in this book are creations
of the author's imagination.
The story is set during the years 1986 and 1987.

CHAPTER ONE

A Snowstorm

School would have to finish early again. Through the classroom windows Tom could see the first few flakes of snow drifting out of the dirty sky. It had been snowing on and off for more than a week now, to the untiring delight of the children and the weary resignation of their parents. Each day there were frantic snowball battles in the playground and riotous tobogganing sessions after school on the slopes behind the church. A succession of snowmen of different shapes and sizes stared silently over the fences of the gardens along the village street. Everyone came home from school soaked at the end of the day, sodden gloves caked with hard snow lumps, cheeks burning, feet freezing. The atmosphere in their homes was like a laundry, a permanent steamy smell of drying clothes.

Tom, Ian and Michael exchanged delighted glances as Mr Nicholls stood up to dismiss the class.

"All those who aren't being collected and where there's someone at home had better go now. It'll be getting dark soon and there's more snow on the way. The rest of you will have to wait. Quietly, quietly please — table by table."

11

Mr Nicholls stood by the door as most of the occupants of each table rose and went down the corridor to the cloakroom. Through the wall the shrill little voices of the infants could be heard in their classroom as they too were getting ready to go home.

"Now you three," Mr Nicholls addressed Tom and his two friends as they hurried gleefully through the door. "Not too many snowballs on the way home. It's getting worse fast, and I don't want any accidents."

"Sir." Tom, Ian and Michael responded automatically, letting the warning float away unheeded.

Outside, they abandoned themselves once more to the breathless delight of pelting one another with the carefully stored ammunition which they had made and piled up behind the bike shed at dinner time. Only when they were all soaked and panting, hands numb inside wet gloves, shattered snowballs spread over their clothes, did they postpone the next round.

"Same time, same place tomorrah, lads!" Michael drawled like a cowboy before turning out of the school gates and charging down the hill, half running, half sliding. Ian and Tom went more slowly, trudging unevenly up the street on the bumpy, tight-packed snow until they reached the turning which led up towards Ian's family's farmhouse on the edge of the downs.

Alone, Tom made his way further uphill along the High Street to the other end of the village where his home, which was also the Post Office, stood. The snow was whirling down fast now; people were hurrying home —

heads bent, collars up. Tom blinked the flakes away as fast as they settled, feather-soft, on his eyelids. It was already blurring the edges of the clumps of old dirty snow piled on the side of the pavement and building up in drifts against the walls of the High Street shops and houses. A few days ago, Tom would have leapt into each unsullied drift; now he passed them without another glance. The snow had come to stay. There was plenty of time.

The lighted windows of the Post Office, tinsel hung and toy-bright ready for Christmas, beckoned him in. His mother was doling out pensions and stamps while his grandmother, stout and sociable, presided over the provisions, newspapers and stationery, hardly pausing in her amiable inconsequential chatter between customers.

"There we are Mrs Hewittson, here's the bacon and I'll just get you a tin of beans... ooh, it's nasty out isn't it — can't keep my hands warm, that's the worst of getting old! Hello Doris! How's your Charlie keeping these days dear? Feeling his age like the rest of us I suppose. Yes, that's five pounds thank you Mrs Hewittson. Cheerio dear. Now what can I get you? Your usual white farmhouse? Yes, I've got it put by — oh look — and here's young Tom home early again. Come on in out of the cold, my pet."

"And mind you wipe your feet," his mother added from behind the Post Office grille. "I don't want all that snow trampled through the house. Go and put the kettle on, there's a love, make Gran and me a cup of tea. We've been so rushed; we haven't had one all afternoon."

"Hi Mum. Hi Gran." Tom wiped his feet with exaggerated care and made his way through the shop to the door at the back which led into their home.

Tom had lived all the ten years of his life in the Sussex village of Fulhurst, which lay in a valley in the middle of the South Downs. The last twenty years or so had seen it grow sideways a bit but it couldn't get much bigger because the downs climbed up behind it so steeply. The river Ful bounded the village on the west side and to the east the downland ridge bumped up and down unevenly southwards towards the Devil's Dyke. In the past many of the villagers had been employed in various capacities by the Warburtons who had lived in Fulhurst Manor since the Middle Ages.

Now there were no more Warburtons, and the Manor had become a Health Spa and Sports Centre, providing a very different sort of employment for many of the locals. The population had changed too; now some of the inhabitants of Fulhurst were incomers — commuters to and from London and Brighton who had bought and restored some of the prettiest old houses in the village. Tom's family, however, was native to that part of Sussex; his mother had grown up in the next valley. When his grandfather died, Gran had come to live with them, so together with Dad and Tom's twelve-year-old sister Julie there were five of them living in the house behind the Fulhurst Post Office and General Stores.

He went into the kitchen, filled the kettle and plugged it in. Always ravenous after the school day, he then wandered about looking for things to eat. There was a large freshly made pie in the fridge, probably for tea later, but Tom resisted the temptation to break off a bit of the crust — it would certainly not go unnoticed. The cake tin yielded him some biscuits and a rather stale piece of chocolate cake — enough to keep him going while he made the tea. Gran liked her tea sweet; Mum had it strong and unsweetened. Tom took advantage of the lack of supervision to make himself a cup just as he liked it best, with four spoonsful of sugar instead of the two he was usually allowed.

When he had taken Mum's and Gran's cups through to the shop he came back and drank his, sitting on the central heating unit, another thing he wasn't supposed to do. It was a lovely cosy place to be, with its heat climbing all the way through him. Tom felt grateful for the pre-Christmas rush, which kept Gran in the shop instead of in here as usual.

As he sipped his tea, a mixture of sad thoughts and happy ones jostled about in his head. On the top was a simple one — eager anticipation for the weekend lying ahead. He, Ian and Michael had planned to take Michael's Dad's old army sledge onto the downs and spend the whole day tobogganing. Ian, who lived on a farm above the village, had asked the other two to lunch, so they could all have a long, glorious day up there without having to go home till tea time.

Pushing into the wake of these plans came a much more depressing reflection. This was the last winter he, Ian and Michael would spend together. Michael's father, who was the local vicar, would be taking up a large parish in Crawley in the New Year. But Ian was going much further afield. His father was selling the farm and the whole family was emigrating across the world to Australia, where Ian's uncle managed a huge sheep station.

To Tom his own life felt boring and unadventurous compared with such plans. He would probably stay in the Post Office till he was grown up, then get a job in the village or round about, as Dad and Mum and Gran had, as their dads and mums had, and so on and so on for years back. School would be much duller without Ian and Michael — they had been his best friends since infant school. They were the Daredevils, the Gang of Three, The Fulhurst Thunderbolts, and lately the Tobogganing Terrorhawks. But there was no fun in being a Terrorhawk on your own. Tom sighed. It would be a solitary spring.

Then a less depressing thought pushed in. There was one bright patch of blue in the leaden grey skies of the lonely weeks and months ahead. Today in school at morning assembly Mr Nicholls had told them all about a big, exciting event being planned for the spring. A theatrical performance using children from schools all over the area was going to be staged as part of a much larger festival. Tom was one of the lucky ones — he would have one of the main parts. The show had lots of music and singing in it; it was a children's opera, all about Noah's Ark. It had originated as a medieval mystery play but had been set to music much more recently.

When Mr Nicholls played them some of the music, Tom had really enjoyed it. He loved singing. A year ago he had become a member of the local church choir, which was why he had been picked to play one of Noah's sons. Lots of school children and grown-ups from places as far away as Lewes and Brighton would be taking part, as well as nearby villages.

It was all happening because Fulhurst Church had been built seven hundred and fifty years ago next March. Over the centuries the church had weathered fires, floods, religious turmoil and all sorts of other disasters — but had survived them all and remained, tranquil and serene, still for many people the beating heart of the village.

The opera had a strange name — 'Noye's Fludde'. Tom thought perhaps that was how Noah's Flood had been written all those hundreds of years ago. Its first performance, with the composer Benjamin Britten conducting, had been in in Suffolk nearly thirty years ago. Mr Nicholls, who was organist and choirmaster at Fulhurst Church as well as being Tom's class teacher, had taken part in that memorable first performance as a small boy.

"I was one of the animals going into the Ark — a rat, in fact," he had told the children that morning. "It was one of the most exciting things I've ever done. I'll never forget it! When I grew up, I thought how much I should like to do it again. Well, of course I'm much too big to be a rat now — but we have plenty of children in this school who are just the right size!" He paused a minute, then added. "It's also very appropriate that we should do 'Noye's

Fludde' here in Fulhurst, because as you know, Fulhurst Church has been flooded many times in its long life, in fact the last time was just over a hundred years ago."

Tom knew that the church had been flooded before because there were marks on the wall both outside and inside, showing how far the water had risen each time. He decided to ask Gran to tell him all about it at teatime; her grandfather had been a little boy at the time of the last flood.

"You're not meant to be sitting there. Gran'll kill you! She's coming through in a minute."

He slipped off his hot but illicit resting place hastily as his sister Julie came in, home from school. He didn't think much of Julie at the moment; she had become far too bossy since she'd started at secondary school. No longer the kind big sister of a few years ago, she spent a lot of time now in her room listening to loud pop music and gossiping with her friends.

Tom sometimes complained about the volume of the music, but she took no notice and also did her fair share of grumbling — when he clumped down the stairs, when he ate his meals and even when he sang in the house. So he didn't tell her about getting the part of Noah's third son, Jaffet, in the play, although he knew she would hear about it sooner rather than later.

"OK, OK — I'm off it now. No need to fuss," he said.

Julie shrugged. "Anything left to eat? I've got to help in the shop for a bit," she added.

Tom indicated the lukewarm tea pot and the remaining biscuits, then heaved a sigh of relief when she disappeared again and was replaced by Gran.

Soon he was telling Gran all about the children's opera while helping her to get the family's meal on the table. It was nice telling Gran things, because she was always interested.

"It's called Noah's Flood, Gran, but it's spelt different, and it's in sort of old-fashioned language. The other sons of Noah are coming from different schools, but they're also in their church choirs. Old Nick — I mean Mr Nicholls — said that's why we three were all chosen, because we sing in our choirs and can read music."

"Oh, then you'll have a lot of singing to do, will you? And acting too. We *are* going to be proud of you, aren't we?" Gran said as she took the meat pie out of the fridge and put it into the oven to heat up.

Tom felt a brief flash of relief that he'd resisted breaking off a bit of the crust earlier; Gran would definitely have noticed and become reproachful rather than pleased.

She went on, busy and cheerful. "Put some bread on the table, will you, love, and get me a packet of peas from the top of the fridge. Will you be dressed up? I could help to make some of the costumes if they had a pattern I could use. I don't know about the animals though; how will they do those, I wonder?"

Tom told the rest of the family his news when they were all sitting round the tea table, knowing that Julie wouldn't dare to make any mocking remarks with three grown-ups at the table.

"'Noye's Fludde' — yes, I think I've heard of it," Dad said as he cut into the steaming hot pie. "Well done lad — lots of solos to sing for the church celebrations eh! We'll be proud of you."

Dad was very keen on anything to do with the church. His day job was as head maintenance operative up at the Warburton Manor Sports Centre, but he was also a churchwarden.

Often Tom found this pretty irksome, there was a lot about the church which he privately thought was extremely boring. But he did love singing. Dad had been delighted when his son got into the choir. It wasn't always easy to please Dad, but tonight Tom had managed it.

Mum joined in the conversation. "I know there's going to be lots of stuff happening this year because of the seven hundred and fiftieth anniversary. The W.I. is planning a big bazaar and a summer fair. You'll be busy, Tom; I expect there'll be other things going on at school too."

Even Julie was interested. "You're ever so lucky, Tom. I wonder if our school is doing anything. Bet it isn't, though. But d'you know what? Mandy Shoesmith said her dad told her that some of the village anniversary celebrations might be televised. Think if you were on telly, Tom!"

That was an exciting prospect; so exciting in fact that they talked of nothing else for quite a time. Tea was nearly over when Tom remembered to ask Gran about the flood in the church when her grandfather was a little boy.

"Oh yes, the great flood. That was an awful business. The river burst its banks and flooded the village. It didn't stay long because the water drained away quite quickly. But three people drowned and there was terrible damage done. Grandpa used to tell us how he looked out of the window and saw chairs and tables and all sorts of bits and pieces from people's homes floating down the village street. And the mud! When the water had drained away there was a dreadful mess of mud all over the bottom end of the village."

"It went into the church, didn't it, Gran? There's watermarks on the wall by the door," Tom said.

"It did, love, the church is right at the bottom of the hill, you see, so it got the worst of it. All the hymn books and prayer books were ruined and lots of the furnishings were spoilt. Grandpa said the village was raising money to repair the church and to replace the spoilt pews and furnishings for years. And groups of ladies worked for months and months making and embroidering new hassocks — there are still a few of them in use in the church today. Funny place to build a church really, mostly churches were built on high ground."

"Yes, this village has been flooded more than once," Mum added. "The 1876 watermarks aren't the only ones in the church. They're just the most recent."

Julie was now as intrigued as Tom. "How often, Mum? And why? Will it happen again?"

"Well, the old stories say so. Hasn't Gran ever told you the tale of the Devil and his curses?"

Gran was about to chip in but Julie, disappointed, responded with a shrug. "Oh that old story. You mean the Devil's Dyke legend. We did that in the first year. It's not just about Fulhurst though, it's about lots of the churches round here."

"Well, I don't know it," Tom said, and Dad turned to Julie with a smile. "Come on then, know-all. Tell us all about it!"

Julie was torn between wanting to stay silent and aloof after being called a know-all, while at the same time keen to show off her knowledge.

"OK then," she said, trying to sound as if it was all rather boring really. "It's about when the first churches were being built around here. People were getting converted to being Christians and the old religions were dying out. The story's about the Devil being angry because he was losing his power, so he started to dig a great big ditch from the sea up to the downs. Then the sea was supposed to rush up and drown all the churches round about. It didn't work, though, 'cos he never finished it — and anyway it isn't true."

Dad nodded at his daughter and added a bit more. "That's right, Jules. The Devil's Dyke down Brighton way is supposed to be the remains of the Devil's ditch — dyke's an old word for ditch, you see, Tom. But the Devil didn't finish it, as Julie says, and I don't think any churches have been flooded that way at all. The floods we've had

22

here in Fulhurst in the past have always been when our river burst its banks, after a storm or suchlike."

Tom turned to his mother. "So, there's no other curse about Fulhurst, Mum, just the Devil's one?"

"Yes, I think there is also an old story, maybe something to do with the Devil's Dyke legend, about a curse on Fulhurst Church. Wasn't it part of the old Abbey when the monks had to move out? Sorry, lovey, that's all I can remember. You'll have to ask Mr Nicholls; I reckon he's better at history than we are. And now it's time we got this table cleared and the washing up done. Julie, haven't you got any homework to do tonight?"

All that talk of floods and curses swished around in Tom's head for the rest of the evening. Every now and then he would glance out of the window at the pale world outside, half-expecting to see the snow all turned to water, rushing in torrents down the village street. But each time he looked the snow was still swirling silently down, the street and the houses lying calm and secret, muffled in white.

Lying in bed later, however, Tom's fears got the better of him. Julie's bored indifference and the grown-ups' matter of fact common sense stayed downstairs with them, while he tossed and turned this way and that, unable to get to sleep.

The wind seemed to be growing wilder all the time. Tom could hear it moaning around the house, finding its way into every unprotected crack of the building, sounding like a lost child wailing. Suddenly Tom sat up abruptly. Surely it wasn't just the wind that he was hearing. There

23

were children out there, sobbing desperately as they dashed through the village, trying to escape a massive tidal wave of water that crashed behind them. Tom nearly cried out for his mother as he had done when he was very little, but even as the panic gripped him, he heard something else which made him think that perhaps the wind really was responsible for all those weird noises after all.

Together with the wailing there was a deep heavy creaking, like a giant walking on loose floorboards. Tom knew what this was. The old apple tree in the garden was protesting under its burden of snow and the assault of the wind. Eerie though this sound was, it comforted Tom because it was familiar. He got out of bed, pulling his duvet around him, and went over to the window. Outside, the night was white with the gleam of fallen snow, and the flakes were no longer dancing down. The wind must have blown away the blizzard, Tom told himself, trying to calm himself down after his fright. Indeed, perhaps the wind itself was fading a little now.

Familiar noises inside the house told him that Julie was now getting ready for bed. He turned away from the window to get back there himself, but before he made it the door opened.

"Tom, what on earth are you doing out of bed?" There was an oblong of yellow light around his mother as she stood in the doorway.

"I couldn't get to sleep, Mum. The wind's so loud."

"Come on, my lad, in you get. Wind's dropping now and the worst of the blizzard's over. Now off you go to sleep, and don't worry, or you'll be too tired to toboggan at the weekend."

Tom climbed back into bed obediently and Mum tucked him in, leaving him with a goodnight kiss and a comforting pat on the shoulder. The wind was dying away, and soon he was sound asleep and untroubled by dreams.

CHAPTER 2

The Man in Black

Of course Tom wasn't too tired to go tobogganing at the weekend. All the new snow had frozen hard and by Saturday morning the sun shone cold and bright out of a clear blue sky. It was a perfect day for winter sports. People said it was more like Switzerland than the South of England.

Newspaper headlines screamed: '**The Big Freeze to go on and on!**' and '**South of England gripped by new Ice Age!**'

Tom and his friends had never known such a winter! They were just about aware that not everyone was enjoying it as much as they were. Tom felt a bit sad when he saw Gran's fingers stiff and swollen, sticking out of the grey mittens she wore in the shop.

Michael, whose father was the vicar, had been pressed into service helping his parents carry extra blankets and hot soup round to some of the old people in the village. Ian's whole household had been upset when, helping his father and elder brother who had spent several hours digging out snowed-in ewes, they found two dead and three others which had miscarried their lambs.

But the boys couldn't concentrate for very long on these more sombre aspects of the big freeze. They were possessed by the snow, punch-drunk with it, utterly enchanted with the new dimension it offered them.

The three of them spent the morning creating a new toboggan run in a field on the slope above Ian's farm. It switchbacked wildly round bushes, rushed over lumps and molehills, bounced across dips and depressions and finally tore down the steepest part of the slope to a flat expanse of deep drifted snow. By lunchtime it was like glass.

"Let's have a Grand-Prix this afternoon!" yelled Ian as they charged into the farmhouse for lunch.

Over baked potatoes and lamb stew they planned the event.

"We'll time ourselves — best of ten," suggested Michael. "No, I know, let's have ten runs each and add up the timings."

"Yeah, then we can see who does the best time of all, as well as the overall winner," said Ian.

"Penalty points for falling off," added Tom. "Say, three seconds each. Only we'll have to leave out Mike's toboggan to make it fair."

His and Ian's were identical; light plastic ones bought from the hardware shop in Lewes. Michael's was much larger and older, heavy and wooden with long curved runners.

Ian's mother, while she dished out stewed apples and custard, announced unexpectedly. "And I'll award a prize to the winner."

"Cor, Mum! Thaa-anks!"

"Ace!"

"Wic-ked!"

After such a huge hot meal the boys felt too full to rush straight back to the field, so they spent the next half-hour working out the framework of their Grand-Prix. Time was to be kept on Michael's digital watch which included a stop-watch. They would rotate the three different jobs — Starter, Racer, and Finisher; each leaving the watch and score sheet at the top of the slope when he turned from Starter into Racer, and taking over the finishing whistle at the end when he turned from Racer into Finisher.

It worked very well. Tom was the first to race. He lowered himself onto the toboggan, breathing in a little extra excitement and tension with the cold air, as Ian, serious faced over the stopwatch, counted down to the start.

"GO!"

Tom pushed off and was immediately skimming the slope like a duck coming down to water. The toboggan leapt over the first of the hillocks, then it was time to tackle the switchback, twisting and swerving down to the finish.

"Great!" Tom landed up in the big snowdrift at the end and tumbled off the half buried toboggan as Michael blew the whistle so Ian could stop the clock. Then Tom took the whistle and Michael set off up the track, dragging the toboggan behind him, to take over from Ian as Starter.

There were some spectacular runs. Ian, scarlet in the face and sitting bolt upright, veered madly off into the trees at a right angle to the track and was lost to view. A succession of Tarzan-like yells heralded his return, as he burst out of the copse and regained the track a bit further down.

Michael turned right over at one point when his toboggan hit a lump under the snow, discharging him into the air. He somersaulted twice before getting the right way up again and racing after the careering toboggan.

By half-time they were all boiling hot, breathless, bruised and battered but tingling with exhilaration.

"Mike's got the best time so far — and the worst," Ian said, looking at the score sheet.

"Not for long!" Tom hadn't had any disasters yet, but nor had he done any spectacularly fast runs. Now that he had the measure of the track he was going to go all out for speed. "You haven't seen my new technique, man! The Human Thunderbolt, that's me."

The Human Thunderbolt came to grief in the same way that Ian had done earlier. Tom tried to gain speed through steering merely by swaying his body from side to side, rather than using his feet. The trouble was that this meant he didn't have much control. When he reached the danger point halfway down the track, he sped off down the rogue diversion through the trees which Ian had carved out when he swerved off-track.

Unlike Ian, though, Tom didn't manage to turn round and get back onto the track. Instead, clinging on grimly to the sides of the toboggan he hurtled along a bumpy and uncomfortable course down a further slope towards a barbed wire fence. Luckily, he managed to slow down before the barbed wire rushed up to grab him. The toboggan turned a half circle and hit a large boulder, tilting on its side and emptying Tom out onto the snow-covered iron hard ground.

"Cor, that hurt!" he gasped as he sat up slowly, bumped and winded and not at all sure in which direction he had been going.

Turning round he saw the crazily twisted tracks of his journey snaking back up the slope towards the trees. One elbow hurt a bit, but neither he nor the toboggan was damaged. Tom got up and righted the toboggan, which was jammed against the huge stone that had stopped its flight. In fact, it wasn't a stone at all, it was part of an old wall, on which Tom now sat to slap the snow off himself and to get his breath back.

"Where are the children?"

Tom, startled, turned round to see a tall man dressed in black like a vicar, standing a few feet away from him on the other side of the old wall and the barbed wire fence. He was no one Tom knew, although for a moment his face looked vaguely familiar. There was something rather alarming about him as he stood there, rigid and dark against the paper-white of the snow. His narrow face was at once stern and sad, set into deep downward lines. The strangest thing about him was his eyes, almost black but with the white showing all around. It was almost as if he had seen something so awful that the horror had become frozen on his face in this unwavering stare, or the horror was stuck inside his own head and he dared not close his eyes for fear of unleashing it. Tom was scared.

"Where are they, the other children?" the man repeated. His voice was harsh.

Tom's voice sounded shrill and unnatural to himself as he started to answer.

"They're just up there, through the trees in the field at the top."

"TOM! Hey, TO-OM!" Thankfully, Tom turned in the direction of the shouting.

"I gotta get back," he said hastily. "COMING!"

He got up quickly, grabbing the string of the toboggan, and began to stamp his way up towards the trees, where he could just make out the moving figures of Ian and Michael behind them. He didn't look back till he was nearly there, then took a quick glance over his shoulder, a bit ashamed of the fear which had overtaken him.

'Probably some old crony of the vicar's, out for a walk,' he told himself, and half raised his hand to wave goodbye. But the man was gone.

Ian and Michael greeted him with shouts of impatience.

"Come on mate, we haven't got all day!"

"Be getting dark soon. Why'd you take so long?"

Tom shrugged his shoulders. For some reason he didn't mention the Man in Black. He didn't know why he said nothing. Michael would have been able to tell him if there were any visitors at the vicarage, and Ian might well have known why there was a stranger wandering round the edge of his father's fields.

"Couldn't stop the blasted thing, then it got stuck," he muttered. "Anyway, let's carry on. But I reckon that's me out of the championship."

It was, too. Michael was the overall winner in the end, but he shared out his prize, a bag of toffees. Tom wasn't sorry when he and Mike left to go home. He couldn't shake off the creepy feeling left by that encounter with the Man in Black. It was only when he got up the next morning that he realised with a thrill of horror why the whole incident had unnerved him so much.

Inside his eyes there was a clear memory of the toboggan track down from the trees. His own footprints too trailed away from the spot, blurred and tangled with the marks of the toboggan when he'd been trudging back to the others. But he remembered that when he had turned to face the man, there had been no tracks in the immaculate white snow of the field behind him; nothing to show where he had come from. As Tom beheld again that pristine expanse of snow in his mind's eye, he didn't want to accept what his memory told him. The Man in Black had left no footprints. He must have been a ghost.

CHAPTER 3

Questions

For the next few days Tom couldn't get the Man in Black out of his head. He went over and over what had happened. Sometimes he tried to reassure himself that he'd been mistaken about the lack of footprints. But every time he succeeded in convincing himself, a picture of that smooth empty white field would flick back into his mind.

However hard he tried to push the disturbing memory of the man away, he couldn't get rid of the image of that haunted, unhappy face. He went over and over what the man had said. What children was he talking about? If he really was a ghost, it couldn't have been Ian and Michael he had been looking for. Perhaps his own children had been lost in the snow long ago and his restless ghost had to keep returning to the place where they had disappeared.

Next time he was at Ian's house Tom tried to make a few casual enquiries.

"Snow's ever so deep in those fields. No wonder the sheep got lost; be quite easy for a little kid to disappear in it too."

"That's right," Ian's mother said. She was piling blankets into a huge cardboard packing case. In a few weeks Ian and his family would be on their way to Australia. She stopped for a moment and smiled at Tom who was still hanging about. "When the boys were small, I didn't let them go in that far field at all after there'd been a heavy snowfall. Mind you, it's not many years you get as much snow as this."

"I wonder if any kids ever got lost down there."

Ian's mother shrugged. "Very unlikely, we'd have heard about it if anyone went missing. Now off you go and find Ian, I need to get this stuff sorted." She had lost interest in the subject.

Tom wandered outside in search of Ian, who was helping his father to shovel soiled straw onto a muckheap.

"Can I help, Mr Hurst?" He grabbed another fork and scooped up a load onto it. "Wonder if the new people have got any kids. Be strange without you lot here."

Mr Hurst was not a talkative man. He nodded his thanks to Tom for his help but didn't say anything. Ian shrugged.

"Dunno."

Tom tried another tack. "Has this always been a farm? Since the olden days, I mean?"

"Mmm, that it has."

Mr Hurst didn't add what he was thinking: not much longer. He was selling the farm and all its stock to start again on the other side of the world. The land would be divided up and sold, the older livestock slaughtered for meat and the young beasts taken to market, and there would be strangers living in the house. He turned to Tom, not wanting to seem too stern despite his gloomy thoughts.

"Yes, surely, lad, always bin a farm here. Used to belong to the Abbey, way back. Then it was run by Warburton tenants. But there's bin Hursts farming here close on a hundred years."

The Abbey! Tom knew of course that there had been an Abbey at Fulhurst hundreds of years ago. The ruins of the Great Church and its side-chapels and outbuildings were on the hill behind the village, jagged and stark against the sky; it was one of the famous sights of the area. Their own village church down by the river had been run by monks from the Abbey, until the Abbey was abandoned, and the monks had to flee when King Henry VIII got rid of the monasteries.

Tom had learnt about it at school, but he hadn't given it any thought since. But now he tried hard to remember what they had been told about Fulhurst Abbey. Perhaps the Man in Black was the ghost of one of the monks. Had his children disappeared when the Abbey burnt down? No, that was a crazy idea — anyway, monks didn't have children; they weren't allowed to get married. So what children was the man looking for? There must, there surely must be some logical explanation for the whole thing. The man was probably just an ordinary but slightly weird bloke, a visitor to the village maybe in charge of a group of kids who he had lost sight of.

Poor Tom. As the days passed and Christmas excitement built up at home and at school, he managed quite successfully to banish thoughts of the Man in Black from his mind. Which made it all the more catastrophic when he saw him again.

CHAPTER 4

Another Visitation

Michael appeared one day just before Christmas carrying a pair of ice skates which had been his mother's when she was a girl. The joys of snow, already beginning very slightly to pall, were abandoned straightaway for the previously unappreciated joys of ice. There was a largeish pond, down in the valley below the Abbey ruins, which had frozen solid as soon as the little stream from the river Ful, which fed it, became ice-bound. Off went the three of them to practice skating there.

It became obvious to Tom pretty soon that skating wasn't going to be one of the things he was naturally good at. They took it in turns trying out the skates, and at first all three of them spent more time falling over than anything else. Then gradually first Michael, then Ian began to master the art of keeping upright. As for Tom, though, whenever his turn came round, he didn't seem to be able to get the hang of it at all. His ankles buckled like limp French loaves every time he tried to stand up, let alone move any distance across the ice. His pride wouldn't let him give up, although by the end of the second day he found himself secretly wishing for a thaw so the lake wouldn't be safe. The only way he managed to move at all was when Ian and Michael slid along, supporting him on either side.

"Come on, Tom, it's easy really". Ian, red faced with the effort of keeping Tom upright, panted encouragingly, while Michael, on the other side, gave some well-meaning advice.

"The thing is, to try and forget about being worried you'll fall over."

Tom, the reddest and hottest of them all, began to lose his temper.

"It's all very well to say stop being worried about falling over but when that's the only thing you ever do — oh — help."

Once more his ankles gave way as he grabbed frantically at his friends, before ending up yet again spreadeagled on the ice.

Privately, Tom was by now thoroughly fed up with skating. He started to dread the daily visits to the lake, so it was a relief when he began to be caught up in the Christmas preparations at church. There were choir practices for the services on Christmas Eve and Christmas Day, as well as carol singing around the village. He opted out of skating and pushed it out of his mind to concentrate on music.

Ian's family were having lots of relatives to stay for this final English Christmas, and Michael was needed at home to help with seasonal preparations at the vicarage, so Tom was determined to put his troubles behind him and concentrate on enjoying all the excitements of Christmas. He was getting rather good at blocking out things that he didn't want to think about. Maybe after Christmas, if the snow was still around, the three of them could get back to tobogganing again for a few last sessions, before both Ian and Michael were gone to their new lives.

It was, therefore, with very mixed feelings that Tom received a bulky parcel from Gran on Christmas morning containing a pair of shiny black ice-skating boots.

"I saw them marked down in that big sports shop in Lewes, darling," said Gran, beaming at him. "I thought 'just the very thing for our Tom, and the right size too!' They're as good as new. We just had to get some new laces and they're all ready for you to go and try."

"Thanks ever so much Gran, they're great!" Tom tried to sound as thrilled as Gran thought he was, but of course his heart sank. Now he really would have to get the hang of skating. Gran would be so disappointed if he didn't use her present. "Great!" he said again. "I'll go down to the pond again tomorrow or the next day and try them out. They'll fit a lot better than Mike's mum's ones."

Perhaps that was the answer — a well-fitting pair of skates. Anyway, with Ian and Mike out of the way there would be no humiliation in his frequent falls. He determined grimly that he was going to get to grips with skating once and for all.

The next morning, he was up in good time. It was a crisp and chilly Boxing Day. The pallid sun glittered frostily in an empty sky as it had done for the last ten days, since the snow had stopped falling. Tom made an early start because he had to be back for lunch; his aunt and uncle and cousins were all coming to lunch for a Boxing Day get-together.

Soon after nine o'clock he was back at the frozen lake — bleak and grey and uninviting. A couple of dejected ducks, looking jaded and moth-eaten at the transformation of their habitat, squatted dolefully among the reeds at the edge. Tom, remembering how miserable they had seemed when he was last there, had brought a pocketful of crusts, which he now flung out over the ice towards them. With greedy quackings they headed for this bounty, making Tom chuckle as he watched their ungainly slitherings across the frozen pond.

It was time, though, to get down to business. He sat on the ground at the edge of the lake, pulled his shoes off and pushed his feet into the skates. They certainly fitted a lot better than the other ones and felt much snugger around his ankles. He laced them up as tightly as he could and stood up slowly, holding onto a small branch which overhung the pond. Perhaps having well-fitting skates would make all the difference.

"Right, here goes," he said to himself, launching himself cautiously onto the frozen pond, first one foot, then the other, taking small fearful steps. Several falls later he had improved slightly, the new skates certainly made

40

things quite a lot easier. He battled on. By now he had forgotten everything except the need to master this irritating sport. He wasn't exactly enjoying himself; he was hot and sweaty; his knees were covered with bumps and grazes under his jeans and his ankles ached. But he couldn't stop now even if he had to. He felt rather as he did when working out a tricky maths problem at school. It wasn't much fun, but it had to be done, and all the pleasure and satisfaction would come after, not during the event.

And at last, *at last*, he really was making progress! With a little thrill of excitement he moved across the pond, sliding from one skate to another in a way that suddenly didn't seem all that far removed from the effortless glide displayed by skaters he had seen on television. Or if not that, at least he was now doing as well as Ian and Mike had done.

"I'm skating! I can do it!" he exulted, giving an impetuous whoop of triumph.

All the more unexpected and shocking, then, was what happened next. As he coasted smoothly towards the other side, a gaunt staring figure reared up in front of him from the tangled mass of bare brown bushes overhanging the pond. It was the Man in Black.

CHAPTER 5

Catastrophe and Recovery

Tom was lying in an unfamiliar bed. His head throbbed and he felt very strange. He couldn't move at all, but his head kept floating off his shoulders and drifting up to the ceiling. How could it do this, when he was stuck in bed, as rigid and straight as the stone figures lying on top of their tombs in Fulhurst Church? He tried to bring his head back again, straining so hard that lots of little spots exploded behind his eyes and welled out of them, running down the sides of his cheeks. Someone came and wiped them away.

"It's all right, darling, have a nice little drink, then you'll be able to go to sleep again."

Tom sipped at the cup which was being held to his lips and floated right away with his head, leaving his whole body behind; eyes closed, hands clasped over his chest, a medieval boy on a stone slab.

Next time he woke up he knew immediately that he wasn't a statue. Only one bit of him had turned to stone and that was his right leg, encased in plaster. Rags of remembrance began to arrive in his mind — his new black skates, ruined forever now because someone had cut the right one away from his damaged foot instead of undoing the laces. Gran would be really upset — she had been so pleased with herself for finding them. He must explain to her; he must tell her that it wasn't his fault the boot had been cut, that he kept asking them not to do it, but they hadn't taken any notice. He would also tell her that he could skate now, thanks to her present, which might cheer her up a bit.

As he went over events in his mind, he remembered how happy he had felt cruising across the pond, triumphant and elated. Why was he now lying in a hospital bed with his leg in plaster?

"The Man in Black," he remembered suddenly, with a gasp of horror. That was how it had happened. When that strange and terrifying figure had confronted him, he had lost his balance and fallen heavily, one leg twisting under him as he hit the ice. In the shock and confusion of the next few moments he had felt no pain, only terror as the apparition stared at him with those appalling, haunted eyes.

"Where are the children?" the man had shouted. "Bring back the children!" and then he was no longer there and Tom was left helpless on the ice, bruised and frightened and in awful pain.

As Tom re-lived those dreadful moments, he could remember hearing and feeling something crack as his legs buckled and he crashed down. He hadn't realised then that it was the snap of some of his bones breaking. But as he tried to struggle up again with a confused idea of following the man, the pain was excruciating. He still couldn't believe that just falling on the ice could have resulted in broken bones, so with the same doggedness which had helped him master the intricacies of skating, he had tried to force himself to get up and off the ice. He fell down again almost immediately, crying out in agony. By now he was shivering with cold as well as with shock and pain. He was surprised at how strange and thin his voice sounded as he began to shout for help.

"Help! Help! I've hurt myself! Oh please, someone come. Help, please come, please come."

As he called, he managed to drag himself along the ice a bit, moaning and panting as he grabbed at the spikes and tufts of grass and reeds sticking through the ice at the edge of the pond. One of the things he noticed was that his gloves were torn and his hands were bleeding, but he was so cold he couldn't feel them hurting at all. Was it hours or only minutes later that he heard a voice calling?

"Hallo! Hallo there! Where are you?" And he could hear someone crunching through the undergrowth towards him.

Only patches of what happened after that had come back into Tom's memory. There was a dog barking and other voices around him. The next thing he remembered was lying in a warm strange room on a sofa with lumpy springs.

At some point he realised his mother was sitting beside him, although he didn't remember telling anyone who he was or where he lived.

"Poor old love," she said, stroking his hair. Tom's eyes overflowed, but he wasn't crying.

"I'm not crying," he said.

"Of course you're not, darling," she responded quickly, and patted him on the shoulder. Then he blacked out again.

Next time he awoke he was in an ambulance, going very fast. He knew it was an ambulance because he was lying on a narrow bed with a red blanket over him, and he could hear the faint sound of the siren behind the other noises of busyness and bustle around him. Everyone was very kind, but no one seemed to understand about the Man in Black, however hard he tried to tell them. His voice seemed to have gone all croaky and weird.

Now, as Tom lay quietly in his firm hospital bed, he felt at last that he had his mind in order again. At this point he decided he would stop mentioning the Man in Black; he was getting better and better at pushing away the things he didn't want to think about. It was a relief to submit to the kindly ministrations of the nurses, to doze and wake and have a drink and doze again. It felt like going back to being a very small child, comfortable, safe and helpless, light years away from the fearful world of frozen ponds and terrifying visitors seemingly returned from the dead.

Tom gradually began to feel rather excited to have his leg in plaster. It hardly hurt at all. There it lay, heavy and white and immobile, like something that didn't belong to him. His mind leapt ahead to a vision of himself at school, having acquired a new, special aura of importance with

45

that stiff smooth leg, and all his classmates clamouring to write their names on it.

When Dave Stockbridge, an older boy, had been knocked over by a car he'd been in plaster for almost a whole term. Tom had envied him with all his heart the glory of that plaster cast, covered all over with drawings and signatures and messages. Still more splendid had been the sight of Dave on his crutches, swinging dashingly down the school corridors and all over the playground. He had become so fast on them that he could even beat some of the other kids when they were running! Tom had yearned to have a go on Dave's crutches; now perhaps he was going to have some of his very own!

"What's your name?"

For the first time since he had started to feel more normal, Tom looked with interest round the ward at the other children, one of whom was standing just beside his bed. He had a shadowy recollection of her being there once or twice before, and that he had then turned away from her and closed his eyes again. He felt friendlier now, so he smiled at her.

"Hello! It's Tom. What's yours?"

"Tracey. I'm seven. I had my appendix out. Have you had an operation?"

Tom wasn't sure whether to say yes or no, he didn't really know, but he was quite happy to listen to Tracey's chatter. It was nice to let her uncomplicated friendliness occupy his attention while he continued striving to blank out the troubling thoughts which lay at the back of his brain. A nurse came and propped him up with pillows against his bedhead then brought a jigsaw puzzle over, which he and Tracey worked on contentedly together, until a clattering noise heralded the arrival of the dinner trolley. Food! He realised suddenly that he was starving! He hadn't had anything to eat for ages, not since the bowl of cereal yesterday morning before he had headed off to the pond with his skates. Was it really only yesterday morning? It seemed like another life.

"What day is it today?" he asked the nurse as she brought him his tray.

"You're looking better!" she said with a smile. "It's Sunday. And here's some dinner for you, I expect you're ready for it!"

Sunday! Christmas Day had been on Thursday, so somehow Tom had lost a whole day of his life. No wonder he was so hungry! The fish fingers and mashed potato tasted quite as good as his Christmas turkey had done four days earlier. With every mouthful he felt the real Tom coming more fully back inside himself. He remembered reading once about food and drink providing 'the restoration of the inner man'. He hadn't properly understood the meaning of this, but now, fortified by food, that very same expression floated into his mind. So that was what it meant!

During the afternoon, a doctor came to see him. He confirmed Tom's hopes about crutches and said a pair were being sent up to the ward.

"When you've got the hang of them, you can go home," he told Tom. "One of the nurses will show you how to manage them."

"Will I go home today?"

"Tomorrow, when I've had another look at you. But you have a go on those crutches this afternoon. It won't take you long to master them."

He was right. When Mum and Julie came to visit later, they saw Tom staggering down the middle of the ward on his crutches.

"Hi Mum; Hi Julie," he greeted them nonchalantly. They were as impressed as he had hoped they would be. Mum was obviously enormously relieved to see him looking so much better.

"What a difference from yesterday!" she exclaimed, hardly able to believe that the washed-out, comatose figure who had lain so still and silent throughout her visit yesterday could have changed back into his old self so quickly. Even Julie was pleased and friendly and presented him with a pocket-sized electronic game she had bought him.

"So, you'll have something to do when you can't go out and play."

"Cor, thanks Jules! It's brill!"

CHAPTER 6

Frustration and Revelation

Tom was discharged the next day, but his visions of himself swaggering up and down the village street on crutches had to wait a while before they could be put into practice. He was shocked and ashamed to find how tiring the crutches proved to be; he found himself having to rest for quite a lot of time each day. Everybody was very kind to him, and Julie's game provided some welcome distraction, but it wasn't long before he realised what a bore it was having his leg in plaster.

The doctor had said it would have to stay on for six weeks, but Tom, wrapped up in dreams of himself as a wounded hero, bearing his plaster and crutches like battle trophies, hadn't really listened to this. But now it began to sink in. Six weeks! Six weeks without running about, without snowball fights, toboggan races — in six weeks there would be no snow left.

There would be no Ian and no Michael either. Tom hadn't thought about his friends much in the past few eventful days, but now he found himself brooding miserably on his misfortune. He wished passionately that he could turn the clock back, that none of this had happened and he, Ian and Michael could still be playing together free and untroubled, without a broken bone between them and the future as assured and secure as the past had been.

The other thing he hadn't anticipated was how very uncomfortable he would be. His leg was heavy and stiff and clumsy, and it often ached unbearably, especially when he tried to get to sleep. Almost worse than the aching was when he got an itch right down inside the plaster where he couldn't get at it to scratch.

He was lying gloomily on his bed regarding the purplish black, bruised toes poking out of the end of his plaster and feeling pretty depressed a couple of days later when Ian and Michael came to visit. At first it was fun. They scrawled their names on his plaster, Michael augmenting his with loops and flourishes in a lurid, lustrous green, and Ian embellishing his with a cartoon of Tom sprawled on the ice. Then Tom demonstrated his prowess on crutches and they both had a go. Julie's game was admired and tried out; they took it in turns to play and had a mini tournament to see who could score the most points. At the same time, the three of them worked their way through the bag of sweets Ian had brought with him.

"Pity about the skates," Ian said, thinking that while Tom's leg would mend, the skate was ruined.

Tom shrugged. He didn't really care. He still couldn't face thinking about that ill-fated day. The memory of the

Man in Black was like a shadow between him and his friends, unmentionable but unforgettable, even more of a barrier than his useless, immobile leg. Michael, slightly ill at ease, then tried to steer the conversation in a different direction, but his choice was an equally unlucky one.

"Dad says Old Nick's planning to start rehearsing the play quite soon, going through all the singing to begin with. It'll be in the church about two weeks after we — or rather you — go back to school. There'll be some grown up singers from Brighton to do Mr and Mrs Noah and the voice of God, and it'll also be you three — Noah's sons — and the girls and boys from other schools, with all the little kids who are playing the animals. You are lucky, Tom; I'd much rather be in the play than moving house."

"Will you still be able to be in it though?" was Ian's hapless enquiry, and in the silence which followed all three of them realised that Tom probably wouldn't. How could he rehearse his part in crutches?

"Well really there's no one else who's a good enough singer," Michael added hastily. "I'm sure Old Nick will want you to do something anyway."

"There's Tony Foley," said Tom flatly. Of course, there was, Tony Foley, that creep!

"Tony Foley is a wally," chanted Ian. "But really, Tom, I mean, he's such a twit, he'd be hopeless."

"Well, no, he wouldn't be, he's a good singer too." Tom had to admit.

"He's the only other person who could sing it. I bet Old Nick asks him. Oh Hell, it's not fair. Of course, he'll have to do it, and he'll be so pleased with himself, it makes me feel sick."

Poor Tony Foley was one of those unfortunate boys whom nobody liked very much. He had ginger hair and lots of freckles, not just on his face but all over his arms and legs too, and had a tremendous temper to go with his fiery hair. Most of his time at school seemed to be spent either in floods of angry tears or clowning around and interfering with everyone's games. He didn't really have any proper friends and was always the person left at the end when they had to choose partners or members of teams in Games.

From time to time he would hang around Ian, Michael and Tom, boasting about things he had done (which they didn't believe) or offering them sweets or stickers if they would let him join in. Sometimes they did; all of them now and then felt the odd pang of guilt about him and from time to time tried to be nice to him. Like Tom, he was in the church choir, where the pair of them were often put together to sing duets. Oddly, when this happened, they seemed to be not merely in musical harmony but more compatible with one another than in any other situation.

At the moment, though, Tom had no room for tolerance or compassion. Fury and resentment had completely taken over; so violent was this feeling that he wanted to scream and smash things up. A year or two ago he probably would have done, but now he managed to control himself until his friends had gone. Then his anger and unhappiness burst out. He flung himself on his bed and cried so much that his pillow had a big wet patch on it and his head ached and ached.

Surely, he must be the unluckiest, unhappiest boy in the whole wide world! Stuck indoors with a broken leg, missing all the fun of the snow and the Christmas holidays, losing his two closest friends at the same time, having to give up his part in the play to someone who was probably the biggest wally in the whole universe... and underlying all this were the horrible visitations of the Man in Black which were so frightening and disturbing that he had to keep them hidden in the deepest recesses of his mind.

He didn't want any tea, so his mother settled him in bed with a hot water bottle and a dose of medicine to ease his throbbing head and aching leg.

But poor Tom couldn't sleep. He was too hot and uncomfortable and unhappy. He lay in the darkened room and felt his eyes overflow again; all his disappointment, pain, anger and fear feeding the flow of tears so they kept rolling out of his eyes and nose. But no one can cry for ever and in the end his tears did dry up, leaving his eyelids fat and heavy and his face stiff and stretched. Drearily he let his eyes close.

He didn't think he would be able to get to sleep but he must have dropped off, because he wasn't in his bed any longer. He seemed to be miles away from everyone and everywhere he knew. There was just himself with his leg, its heavy white bulk showing up ghost-like in the darkness. He lay on the open ground of a grey moor, all alone. The dusky sky above him was moonless and starless, and the only thing he could see across the stretch of moorland was a high grassy bank, denser than the sky, stretching across the horizon. Although it filled him with dread, he knew he must get up and go towards it. He must climb over it and look down at the huge expanse of water which he knew lay on the other side, menacing and silent, waiting for him.

Tom started to get up and jerked himself into wakefulness as he did so, realising that he couldn't go anywhere because of the leaden inertness of his leg.

It was a relief to have got away from that dismal place, but Tom was afraid he would be there again the instant he let himself go back to sleep. At first it was easy to stay awake, because he had woken so suddenly that everything felt jangled and alert, but gradually the ragged patches of sleep behind his eyes started to join together again.

He was back by that terrible motionless stretch of water, but suddenly it boiled up and burst over the grassy bank, rushing at him, crashing and roaring through the village. Panic-stricken, Tom knew that it was because of him that it had been released and was pouring headlong though the village to drown all the children. And he knew he had to save the children. The Man in Black had told him so.

"I'm asleep. It's a dream." Tom was saying in his head as he struggled not only to escape from the rushing water but also to shake himself out of his nightmare. He thought he must have succeeded, because now he was back in his bedroom, standing by the window looking down at the village street. There was no water, only the pearly luminous gleam of snow lying on people's rooftops and in

54

their front gardens. The snow, together with the glow of streetlamps along the pavement, spread an unearthly light over the silent scene. Then, as Tom watched, he saw a boy walking slowly down the empty street. He wasn't anyone Tom knew, and he was playing a pipe as he walked. Tom's ears, which had been full of the gushing sounds of water, were suddenly empty. There was no noise except the high thin sound of the pipe.

As the boy passed below Tom's window he looked up. Their eyes met, and for a second Tom had an extraordinary sensation of insight and understanding, as if all the questions which had no answers were about to become clear to him. But nothing happened, the moment passed and with it the boy, taking his secrets and Tom's nightmare away with him.

The tune stayed with Tom, haunting and unforgettable, echoing round his head, and calming and comforting him so he slept deeply and dreamlessly until morning.

CHAPTER 7

A Dilemma and a Decision

It wasn't much of a surprise to Tom when Mr Nicholls came to visit him two days later. Tom suspected he knew why he had come. There were a few polite preliminaries to be dealt with first.

"How's the leg? That's a pretty smart plaster you've been fixed up with. Can I draw something on it?"

"OK." Tom agreed without enthusiasm.

He was embarrassed as well as irritated by Old Nick visiting him at home. When he was younger, Tom had thought that the teachers all lived at school and had their tea and breakfast there as well as their dinner. Of course, he now knew that teachers, just like anyone else, had families of their own and homes to go to, but Old Nick didn't really seem to belong anywhere but at school or at choir practice in church. He looked out of place to Tom, sitting here on the sofa in the lounge, with Gran's sewing bag slumped beside him and a Royal Wedding mug of tea in his hand.

On the mantelpiece there was a photograph of a three-year-old Tom sitting on Gran's lap. He wore blue corduroy dungarees with an orange elephant on the front and held a bedraggled toy rabbit known as Yabby, who had accompanied him to bed every night until he was nearly eight. Would Mr Nicholls notice it? Even worse, had he seen Julie's copy of the magazine 'Jackie' splayed out on the floor beside Tom's chair, and would he think Tom had been reading it? (Actually, Tom had, but he wouldn't want Old Nick to know that!). But Mr Nicholls seemed completely unaware of these potential causes of shame. He bent over Tom's leg and started to scribble a stylish little drawing on it, depicting Tom dashing along on crutches with a hugely bandaged leg.

"Cor, that's good, sir," Tom said, admiration covering his self-consciousness for a moment.

"Show me how well you're managing to get about on them, it looks rather fun."

"OK." Tom, feeling just a bit more friendly now, pulled his crutches over and stood up. It was, after all, quite nice to have an opportunity to show off his new-found skill to someone.

As the doctor had predicted, he'd quickly become quite an expert. His latest achievement was leaping over small pieces of furniture rather in the manner of a pole-vaulter.

"There's not much room in here, but I can go pretty fast outside, especially when they've gritted the pavement. D'you want to see?"

"Well, not now I don't think; there isn't really time. But I'll look out for you in the playground next week. Don't you find it makes your arms ache a bit? I remember when I broke my knee at college and had some crutches, I got really sore places under my arms from using them so much. Of course, they were a more old-fashioned model, I think modern ones like yours are much more comfortable."

Tom was intrigued to hear this. How had Old Nick broken his knee?

"Did you slip on the ice, like me?"

"No, it was in the summer. I was fielding in a cricket match, but I wasn't wearing pads, and the ball smashed right into my knee. Oh, it was agony! And I was furious, because I was in the First Eleven and it was the beginning of the season. I had to miss all the other matches. I thought they couldn't possibly manage without me. They did, though."

At this moment Tom became aware exactly where this conversation was going. Old Nick had reached the point which he had come here to make. With a return to his sullen manner Tom made it for him.

"Like I suppose 'Noye's Fludde' can manage without me?"

"Well, that wasn't quite what I was going to say. But OK, let's not beat about the bush any longer. That broken leg of yours is going to make it much more difficult for you to play Jaffet; he has lots of rushing about, building the Ark, helping with the animals, and so on — but it would still be technically possible for you to do it. After all, the show's not till March and you'll be out of plaster by then."

Tom was amazed and delighted. He hadn't expected this!

"Oh, great, sir, I'll work really hard at it so when after they take my plaster off—"

"Just a minute, Tom, I haven't finished. As I said, it isn't impossible for you to carry on doing Jaffet, but it's going to make everything a lot more complicated, not just for you but for the rest of the cast too. There's also the risk that after six weeks in plaster the bones haven't yet finished healing and you need a week or two longer — that could take us up towards the end of February. And since we do have someone else in the school who could do the part—"

Tom's mouth suddenly tasted as if a gulp of sick had come up into it.

"Tony Foley."

"That's right, Tony Foley. No, listen, Tom." — for Tom was about to interrupt. "Look, Tony's got to learn the part anyway, because he's the understudy. We both know he would do it very well; in fact, it was touch and go which of the two of you would get it. In the end I opted for you, as being more reliable, with him as understudy. But we can easily reverse those roles, which in any case could mean you'd probably still get the odd performance if he had to miss one. It could also be a chance for Tony to prove himself. He doesn't have an easy time of it at school and this might well make a lot of difference to him. There's nothing like being in a play to help people get on with one another, and it would be a very generous thing for you to

59

agree to. But it's up to you, Tom. If you really feel you can't bear to give it up, so be it. On the other hand, there's something else which I think only you, of all the Fulhurst children, would be capable of doing."

During this speech Tom's indignation had been steadily expanding. What sort of a dirty trick was Old Nick going to play next? First to raise his hopes by saying he *could* do Jaffet after all, then to appeal to his 'better nature' by suggesting it would be good for Tony's confidence to let him take the part, and lastly to try and win him over with flattery. Well, Old Nick wasn't going to get his way. Tom's 'better nature' wasn't going to be given the chance to consider the request, nor was he going to be bribed into doing whatever the other thing was that Old Nick wanted him to consider. He said nothing.

Mr Nicholls tried again.

"I'd like you to have a look at this descant recorder part. It's pretty tricky but very important, and we *were* going to get someone from another school. But the more Fulhurst children we can use, the better. What do you think?"

Tom refused to look at him.

"I still want to do Jaffet."

Mr Nicholls got up to go.

"OK, fair enough. But do have a look at the music anyway. If by any chance you do change your mind you can let me know in a day or two. Oh yes, one other thing. I assume you'll be at choir practice this evening. I want you to do the Epiphany Anthem with Tony. You know it, it's the one you did last year, with shared solos and duets

60

in counterpoint. It's the vicar's last Sunday here so we want to give him a good send-off with lots of nice music."

'Yet another demand,' Tom thought sourly. But he knew Dad wouldn't hear of him backing out of that one, so he agreed in a very begrudging tone of voice.

When Mr Nicholls had gone Tom picked up the recorder part and flung it over to the other side of the room. No way was he going to be a weedy old recorder player instead of one of the most important people in the play. No way was that dummy Tony going to play his part. No way was he even going to look at the recorder music. And he would tell Old Nick so at choir practice.

Every time Tom thought about it all during the next few hours his sense of injustice boiled up again. He arrived at church for choir practice that evening simmering with anger, and proceeded to glower his way through the anthem and hymns. To make things worse, Tony Foley looked so pleased with himself that Tom was convinced someone must have told him he might get Tom's part. Tom wanted to smash that reddish freckled face in, as Tony smirked complacently from the opposite pew. He had to be content with glaring at Tony and sticking his tongue out or making a face at him every time Old Nick's back was turned. No one, listening to the two boys rehearsing their solos and shared duets in the anthem could have guessed at the currents of hostility buzzing between them. Their voices rose together in angelic harmony while their faces exchanged silent messages of hatred.

After choir practice Tom spread his face with a bland expression of wide-eyed innocence and made his way over to Mr Nicholls.

"Please, sir, I really do want to keep on doing Jaffet. I've thought about it a lot and I think—"

But Mr Nicholls didn't seem very interested in explanations. He didn't even look at Tom but nodded as he collected the anthem copies.

"OK Tom. Let me have the recorder part back on Sunday, will you. 'Night, all, don't be late on Sunday."

Tom limped triumphantly down the aisle to the door of the church. That should keep old Tony in his place! He took a swift glance over his shoulder. Tony's face was redder than ever, and he looked as if he was going to cry. He grabbed his anorak and dashed past Tom and out of the church. Tom had won!

But incredibly, by Sunday Tom had completely changed his mind. It was a hard and painful decision to make, and he didn't even have the private satisfaction of feeling he had been benevolent to Tony, because Tony didn't come into it at all. Something happened which persuaded him that playing the recorder was what he was meant to be doing. It was another of those things which didn't seem to have any explanation; another piece of the strange mystery which had been thrust upon him by the Man in Black.

CHAPTER 8

Acceptance

On Sunday morning after breakfast Tom looked for the recorder part of 'Noye's Fludde' to give back to Mr Nicholls. He hadn't seen it since he had flung it away furiously after Old Nick's visit two days earlier. In the end he found it, tidied away by Mum, on the shelf in his bedroom where he kept his recorder. Just out of curiosity Tom decided to see how hard the part really was. He picked what looked like a fairly straightforward bit to start with and began to play. The recorder sang out high and clear, in a tune which sounded oddly familiar to him; in fact, he found he knew what it sounded like even before he played the notes.

He had heard some bits of 'Noye's Fludde' when Old Nick had played them parts of the piece, the bits where Noah and his children were building the Ark, near the beginning, and then the part when the animals were processing into the Ark, but this tune came later. Could he have heard it without realising what it was, sometime at school? All at once a picture came into his mind, a picture of a boy walking along a frozen street playing a pipe. Of course he knew the tune, it had been singing in the back of his head for days. It was the tune that the boy in his dream had been playing. In his memory's eye Tom saw the boy clearly again, looking up at him. And he realised that the boy's face was very like his own.

"So, what the hell's that supposed to mean?" Tom asked himself.

He puzzled over it all the way through the service, blind for once to the irritating presence of Tony in the opposite pew. He joined in the hymns without thinking about what he was doing and sang his solos and his parts of the duet in the anthem with his attention miles away. It was an easy enough piece anyway; his voice remembered it from last year.

"God wants us to look for deeper meanings in everyday things," the vicar said in his sermon, beginning to talk about the gifts of the Three Kings. "A gift is not just an object; it has a more profound meaning too. God's messages to us are not all about great mysteries, strange occurrences, miracles and moving stars in the sky."

Tom couldn't bear to think that the weird things which had been happening to him, ordinary and extraordinary, were part of God's plan. He wasn't even sure that he believed in God anyway. Really, he only went to church because he was in the choir and because Dad insisted on it. There were lots of things which made him think that there might not be a God, because of all the bad things that happened — the bomb, for instance, and cancer, and starving people, and terrorism, and wars. Tom found it easier to believe in ghosts than in the Holy Ghost, easier to believe in magic than in miracles.

When he was younger, he had accepted without question the existence of Father Christmas, and once he was sure he had actually seen the sleigh and the reindeer disappearing into the cloudy night sky. Now he knew that there was no Father Christmas, and that he must have imagined or dreamed that sighting. But he still remembered it vividly.

Tom and his friends loved ghost stories. Everyone seemed to know someone who had seen, or at least heard tell of a ghost. The supernatural seemed pretty real to them all. Now, to Tom, it was more real than ever before. Whatever mysterious influence it was that had taken a hand in his affairs — whether it was God, or Allah, or Vishnu, or Buddha or any other of the mystical figures they had learnt about in school, it didn't matter. What he began to realise was that it wasn't going to leave him alone. He had started to become aware of a sort of pattern emerging.

First there had been the night of the blizzard, before the Christmas holidays. That was when he'd thought he heard children crying and water crashing through the village. Had that, though, just been his imagination working overtime after Gran's account of the 1876 flood?

The Man in Black, however; that had been no flight of fancy. It had been on a day of action, the day of their tobogganing Grand-Prix. Any fantasising he might have done then had been concentrated on seeing himself as a world bobsleigh champion. And then, with no warning, he had come face to face with that terrifying apparition which had put paid to his peace of mind from that day onwards.

"Where are the children!" the man had shouted at him. Always children, lost children. What children were they, and what had it all got to do with him, Tom Lulham?

The next experience had convinced him that for some reason it definitely did have something to do with him. This was the nightmare in which he himself had somehow been involved in the unleashing of the flood which was going to drown all the children. Then he had seen and heard the boy with the pipe. Who was that boy? Was he doing something Tom was meant to do? Was he, indeed, an image or even an ancestor of Tom himself? Why was he playing Tom's recorder tune? Tom would have given a great deal not to believe any of it, but it had all gone too far now. Furthermore, he had a horrible feeling that many more strange things were going to happen to him before it was all over.

Tom felt a bit like one of the small plastic Playmobil people he used to play with when he was little. According to his ideas for any game he planned, he had selected figures and shifted and lifted and manipulated them, so they fulfilled whatever he demanded of them. Now he imagined himself being chosen by a huge invisible giant to be the main actor in a bizarre frightening game. He was being pushed around and being subjected to all sorts of scary experiences, including having his leg broken, in order to play out a story he didn't understand at all.

Turning his back and pretending everything was normal didn't work any more. He had to play his part. It was a disturbing realisation.

"Why me? Why does it have to be me?" raged poor Tom to himself.

But apparently it did have to be him. For some reason he had to be on hand to do something which would avert a terrible catastrophe. So that was that. If breaking his leg and not being able to do Jaffet, and therefore being available to play a particular tune on his recorder was going to make a difference, if this was somehow going to influence what might or might not happen, maybe he should be prepared to take up the challenge. He decided to tell Old Nick he had changed his mind.

Strangely enough, after all that anguish and soul-searching, once Tom had made this decision, he felt quite a lot better. He also found some reassurance in thinking about that mysterious pipe-playing boy, who seemed as if he might be a sympathetic influence in whatever trials and challenges lay ahead.

So, with a slightly lighter heart than previously, Tom shelved his troubles for the time being and started to look forward to the big party which was to take place in the village hall that evening. It was a farewell celebration for the vicar and his family, and everyone in the village had been invited.

Tom resolved to have a good time after the emotional roller-coaster of the last few days. He joined in all the festivities with determined enthusiasm, keeping out of

Tony Foley's way and avoiding Old Nick who had been embarrassingly pleased with him at his decision over the play. With Ian and Michael, he ate an enormous amount of food including barbecued chicken legs, sausages, crisps, jelly, trifle and cake, washed down with as much fizzy fruit juice he could drink.

There were party games, prizes, dancing and even a firework display outside the village hall. It was a riotous evening, ending with an emotional farewell to Michael's father and his family, delivered, with a presentation, by Mr Nicholls on behalf of the village, the church and the school.

When it was all over Tom followed his family home, limping up the dark, cold street. He felt very tired but elated too. Nothing had really changed. Ian and Michael would both be gone in a few days. He was still on crutches with his leg in plaster, and he was no longer playing Jaffet. But an adventure lay ahead of him. There might be dangerous and fearsome times in store, but like the heroes of old, he had undertaken an unknown challenge, and for the time being at least, his mood was buoyant and bold.

Unfortunately, this optimistic frame of mind didn't last very long. It was swiftly dispelled by the return to school the next day.

CHAPTER 9

Rebellion

"Hiya, Tom!"

Tony Foley was hanging about near the school gates when Tom arrived on the first day of the new term. He was grinning in his usual annoying way. Tom didn't want to talk to him, but Tony came down the path with him.

"It's great that I'm doing Jaffet, you know. I mean, I'm sorry about your leg and all that, but—"

Tony was the last person Tom wished to see, and Jaffet the last thing he wished to talk about.

"Get out the way, Tony, I need more space." This wasn't really true, but he tried to take up the whole path as he swung along it on his crutches, forcing Tony to drop back.

"OK, OK, you don't have to be so grumpy. Hey, can I have a go? They look great!" This attempt at reconciliation was not welcome.

"No. Leave me alone."

"Just 'cos I've got your part. 'S not my fault you smashed your leg up. Anyway, Old Nick reckons I'll do it really good."

Tom's patience was being tried very hard. He couldn't and wouldn't tell Tony the real reason he had given up the part. But while he still knew he had made the right, indeed the only possible decision, to have Tony crowing about all Tom had lost was like ripping a scab off an unhealed sore. He couldn't resist giving a taunting retort.

"Bet you don't. Bet you make a real mess of it. Anyway, who wants to sing? Dear little Tony, singing all the solos to the mummies and daddies, what a sweet little boy!"

Tony started to go pink, a sure sight of his swelling anger. His face, spotted with freckles, pushed up close to Tom's.

"You watch it, Tom Lulham."

Tom stuck one of his crutches out as Tony came near, and tripped him up, then made as quick a getaway as he could down the rest of the path into school. Behind him came Tony's roars of rage and pain. When Tony entered the classroom, pink and dishevelled, his hair sticking up and his eyes red-rimmed, Mr Nicholls was taking the register and Tom was sitting decorously at his desk.

'Round one to me,' thought Tom with satisfaction.

This satisfaction didn't last long. The classroom seemed hollow without Ian and Michael. Although everyone crowded round him and wanted to try out his crutches and write on his plaster cast, as the day wore on Tom began to feel as isolated as Tony was. However interesting and novel his broken leg seemed to everyone, in the end it was he and he alone who had to cope with being on crutches. He'd never thought about being left behind before, but now he was last whenever they moved around, from classroom to assembly, from dinner hall to playground.

It was no fun struggling along the corridor to the gym to spend half an hour watching the rest of his class bouncing around on the PE apparatus. It was no fun limping morosely around the playground on his own, having to be careful in case he fell down, like an old man. Even a visit to the lavatory had become a complicated manoeuvre instead of the unconsidered fragment of the day it should have been.

Everyone was eager to help, but he hated the feeling of dependence. If Ian and Michael had still been around, it would have been different.

"I'll get your dinner, Tom," said Amy, who was standing next to him in the queue.

"Need any help on the stairs, Tom?" asked Mrs Antrim, the infants' teacher, as he made his laborious way down to the hall.

"Shall I get your coat down?" offered Craig, whose peg was next to his own.

He refused as much help as he could manage without, but managing was a dreary business. No football, no swimming, no PE, just patches of hanging about between work and play periods throughout the week like a series of blanks.

By Friday he was absolutely fed up. He came into school determined to cause trouble. To start with he pulled Tony Foley's jacket off its peg and kicked it with his crutch all over the muddy cloakroom floor, leaving it in a heap inside the boys' toilets. At playtime he amused himself by grabbing the bobble-hats off some of the infants and flinging them into a heap of dirty snow piled by the caretaker's hut. Back in the classroom, during a Topic session he deliberately upset a jar of paint water over the table, spoiling everyone's work including his own. When he sat for half an hour staring at a blank piece of paper during Maths Mr Nicholls finally lost patience with him.

"For goodness' sake, Tom Lulham, what's got into you today? I thought you'd broken your leg, not your head. Get on with your work, and let's have no more nonsense!"

"'S a load of rubbish, Maths, anyway," said Tom loud and clear, and swept his book, pencil, paper and ruler onto the floor.

He was in that rare state of total defiance where he didn't care what might happen to him. The class sat still and held its' collective breath, agog, expectant.

"Get out!" said Mr Nicholls. "Just get out. Wait outside Mrs Clarke's room till the bell goes. I will not have you disrupting the class any longer."

Mrs Clarke was the headmistress. Tom hung himself on his crutches and swept out through the door which a stony-faced Mr Nicholls was holding open for him. He heard the door slam shut again as he made his way down the corridor to the row of chairs lined up outside Mrs Clarke's office.

When he got there, he decided not to stay. Mrs Clarke was a great one for trying to understand, trying to get children to talk about their anger and often suggesting reasons for their bad behaviour which seemed to have nothing to do with whatever crime had been committed. Tom didn't want to be psychoanalysed. He was in trouble already; he might as well make it real trouble while he was about it.

Moving as quickly as he could, he headed to the cloakroom and grabbed his parka and rucksack. A minute or so later he bounded towards the school gates as fast as his crutches could carry him. He had escaped!

At first, he thought he might go up the hill at the back of the school and hide in the tumbledown shed which he, Ian and Michael had used last summer as the headquarters of the Fulhurst Thunderbolts. But the downs looked bleak and uninviting in their shroud of snow and would be hard to reach too in his current lame state. Anyway without Ian and Mike it wouldn't be much fun.

As he hesitated, the Brighton bus came along the street heading towards the middle of the village. Instantly Tom knew exactly where he was going. In his pocket were two bright chunky pound coins, a Christmas gift from his aunt, and more than enough to get him to Brighton and back. He hailed the bus and heaved himself onto it, his heart beating faster than usual with a mixture of guilt and exhilaration. Would anyone ask why he wasn't at school?

The driver did. He recognised Tom immediately; his two kids were also at Fulhurst CE Primary.

"Yes, well, the doctor says I can go back on Monday," Tom lied glibly. "Brighton return, the Old Steine please. I'm meeting my dad there."

Without further comment the driver gave him his ticket and change. Tom relaxed into his seat, feeling the heat of his lies die slowly out of his face, but nevertheless uneasy that someone else might recognise him.

Each time the bus stopped he gazed fixedly out of the window with his back turned to the entrance. He could still be discovered. Supposing, for instance, Mrs Hookham from the garage got on. She made no secret of her dislike of most boys and her conviction that they were nearly always up to no good. Tom couldn't stop his mind rushing into an imaginary conversation with her.

"Morning, Mrs Hookham."

"I thought you were going back to school with the rest of them, young man."

"Monday, the doctor said. I'm going down Brighton to meet my dad."

"If you can take a bus to Brighton you can go to school."

"It's not like that, Mrs Hookham, you see, I'm going to the dentist, Dad's taking me."

"There's a perfectly good dentist in Lewes. I don't believe you. I think you're playing truant."

"Oh no, Mrs Hookham."

Grave, unsmiling, Tom imagined himself looking at her straight in the face, the innocent boy wronged by a spiteful old lady. A hint of righteous indignation would mingle with the hurt in his voice. Tom could almost feel the pain of an aching tooth as he explored his mouth with his tongue. He dismissed Mrs Hookham as swiftly as he had conjured her up and spent the rest of the bus ride imagining conversations with other spirits whom he summoned from the village.

To Mum he said that Mr Nicholls had sent him on the bus as part of a class survey on public transport. To the vicar (Mike's dad, who persisted in jostling his way into Tom's consciousness even though he and his family were now living in Crawley) he said that he had an appointment at the fracture clinic. That was a good one! It would do much better than the other stories. He enlarged on the theme and began to tell his imaginary audience how neither Mum nor Gran could leave the shop, so Dad was meeting him in Brighton and taking him up to the hospital.

It was to check the X-rays of his foot, he decided; they needed to do something to his plaster. All at once a real voice sent all the phantoms back into thin air.

"Come on, old son, this is where you get off."

They had arrived at the Old Steine.

Brighton was like a different world. The snow had disappeared from the streets but was still spread over the Pavilion Gardens, and the Pavilion itself with its domes and pinnacles looked like an ice palace in a fairy-tale. From the Old Steine Tom headed for the sea front. Like the Pavilion it was transformed; with its familiar yellow shingle hidden under a glittering carpet of powdery white snow.

To Tom, who knew Brighton beach practically as well as his own back garden, it was a chilling sight, as if the whole area had become part of a different coastline. The view out to sea made him think of a black and white photograph: a pale sky overhead, with the two piers stretching like a pair of long dark claws over the colourless beach into the leaden grey water. Tom shivered. It was cold and a bit creepy. He turned back towards the town centre, friendly and colourful with twinkling lights and crowds of people shopping in the January sales.

His spirits rose as he made his way to the Lanes, enjoying the eager bustle around him and elated by a sense of freedom and escape. Tom was rather surprised at himself for feeling so light-hearted. Bunking off school was not something he made a habit of doing. In fact, he had only done it once before, as a dare with Ian and Mike about a year ago. Then, they hadn't been able to relish their stolen liberty with much enjoyment; fear of discovery had sent them back before their absence had even been noticed. But this time Tom didn't care, he had left his guilt behind on the bus.

He grinned at passers-by as he negotiated the narrow, cobbled street. Some of them smiled back at him; he read sympathy for his lameness in their glances. The brave disabled boy, struggling against the crowds, that was who he was, with a smile for everyone, making light of his troubles.

As he passed the multi-coloured shops, their windows shrieking '**SALE**', he incorporated them into a new fantasy. The angular supercilious dummy models draped with clothes were a crowd of snooty women, intent on catching him and sending him to an orphanage. But he managed to creep past them and found his escape in the next window, which had a display of globular lampshades like a flight of balloons. Tom sent his pretend-self up into the sky with them and paused while he considered the next stage of the game and rested his leg for a bit, leaning against a shelf of books outside a second-hand bookshop.

"Look out! You'll have all those over in a minute."

Tom turned quickly as the shelf shifted behind him. A man had come out of the shop with an armful of books and stood looking at him.

"Go on, move yourself, I've got to fit all these in."

"Sorry." Tom shuffled to one side, and to prove he wasn't loitering, abandoned his daydreams and started to look through the row of books. It was pretty boring stuff on the whole: 'Recipes from a Country Kitchen', 'Planning and Maintaining an Orchard', 'Wandering through the Weald'… But what was this? 'Sussex Ghost Stories'. Tom thought immediately about the Man in Black. He picked up the book, feeling a mixture of dread and curiosity, and started to look through it.

This book was fascinating! There were phantom highwaymen, spectral maidens, mermaids and sea monsters, and supernatural smugglers. There didn't seem to be any mention of the Man in Black. Tom felt relieved and decided to treat himself to a helping of spine-chilling escapism.

"How much is this?" he asked the shopkeeper, who had emerged from the shop again with more books.

He took it from Tom and leafed through it. It wasn't in very good condition; some of the pages were loose and it looked as if it had been stained with ink around the spine.

"You can have it for thirty pence, son." Now that Tom had become a customer the man was much more friendly.

"I'll take it."

Tom handed over the money and headed off down the street. He'd bought a return ticket on the bus, and the book had cost him thirty pence, but he had enough money left for a portion of chips and a fizzy drink in a nearby café. It was lovely to get out of the cold, to rest his leg, to luxuriate in the warm steamy atmosphere of the café and to sniff hungrily at the savoury aroma of frying food. Soon the chips arrived, hot and crispy. Tom squirted ketchup lavishly over them, took a gulp of his drink, and started to read about the Phantom Wreckers of Bodle Point.

About twenty minutes later his plate and glass were empty. He was hardly aware of having eaten or drunk after that first delicious shock to his taste buds, so engrossed was he in the Sussex Ghosts. From wreckers and smugglers, he went to highwaymen, from highwaymen to soldiers, from soldiers to mermaids, from mermaids to monks.

Monks! There were plenty of accounts of ghostly monks haunting chapels and graveyards, but no mention of Fulhurst. But Tom's feeling of relief was premature. Over the page was a list of the monasteries in Sussex which had been abandoned during the reign of Henry VIII and which had ghost stories associated with them. And there, halfway down the list, was Fulhurst.

'Fulhurst Abbey, near Lewes, was run by monks of the Benedictine order' he read. 'It was so badly burnt after the Dissolution that it was never used again. During the seventeenth century it became part of the estate of the Warburton family, to whose gifts were also added the livings of the three local village churches formerly administered by the Abbey. For the Fulhurst ghost story, see page 193.'

Tom's heart began to beat uncomfortably. But of course, he felt compelled to find out more. Nervously he turned to page 193. As soon as he saw the title of the chapter his feeling of dread deepened. It was called 'Ghostly Children'. With his head full of fear Tom read on.

'There is an intriguing story of not one, but at least a dozen ghostly children connected with the parish church at Fulhurst. In the winter of 1687 the river Ful burst its banks and flooded the village, drowning more than twenty people, including several children, who were trapped in the church during a Twelfth Night service. The day the village buried its dead the twelve drowned children were seen climbing the hill behind the village towards the ruins of the old Abbey, deserted a hundred and fifty years previously. They were being led by a tall man wearing a black Benedictine habit. Matthias Bysouth, Rector of the church between 1865 and 1890, refers to this event in his 'History of the Abbey of Fulhurst', published in 1893.'

Slowly Tom closed the book. Despite the warm stuffiness of his surroundings, he felt cold again, chilled from the core of his body to the surfaces of his clammy hands. So this was the meaning behind his nightmares. This was the truth about the Man in Black. Swiftly behind the sickening realisation that his ghosts were real came more fear and confusion. There was still so much he couldn't understand. Why, for instance, was the monk leading the children to the Abbey? Was he a still older ghost, one of the monks who had been expelled from the Abbey well over a century before? Had all this been part of the curse? There was nothing about a curse in this account, but Gran and Mum had talked about one. Tom knew there would be no peace for him now until he had uncovered the whole story.

He stood up, stiff and cold, shivering as he limped out of the café. The noisy brightness of the town, so cheerful and stimulating when he had arrived, now seemed tarnished and alien. He wanted to go home, back to the secure familiarity of the Post Office, back to the real world, despite the scolding he knew would be in store for him when he arrived. Facing his parents after playing truant from school seemed a small, safe, everyday thing compared to the horrors which flapped round inside his head. As if in a trance he headed for the bus station and caught the next bus home. His rebellion was over.

CHAPTER 10

Consequences

"Here he comes now." Tom heard his mother say as he walked in through the door from the Post Office.

There was quite a reception committee awaiting him: Mum, Dad, Gran, and Mr Nicholls. Julie was in the shop. As he had passed her, she'd given him an expressive glance, mingled sympathy and curiosity. He'd shrugged his shoulders with uneasy bravado and went on in to face them all. It was later than when he usually got home from school, and it was obvious that they had all been sitting there for some time, by the evidence of the empty teacups and the warm stuffiness of the room.

Dad's face was very stern. Tom glanced round at Mum, who looked distressed, and at Gran, who couldn't help giving him a small rueful smile of welcome. Lastly, there was Old Nick, standing with arms folded, regarding him with the eyebrow-raised, sardonic expression Tom knew well and didn't like at all. He took a deep breath and plunged straight in.

"I'm sorry, sir. I bunked off to Brighton. I was in a really cross temper. I'm ever so sorry."

"We know where you've been," said Mr Nicholls. "Mrs Hookham from the garage saw you and very kindly rang the school. She heard you asking for a return ticket, so we knew you'd be coming back."

So she had seen him after all. She must have been on the bus all the time, nosy old bag — but somehow Tom couldn't muster up the hostile feelings he'd had earlier. After all, if she hadn't made that phone call his family would have been really worried and they would probably have called the police, which would have made everything even worse than it already was.

He hung his head as Mr Nicholls continued to speak.

"Basically, it saved us a lot of worry and trouble. At least we knew where you were, and that you'd be back. But let me make it absolutely clear from the start that you've been neither very clever nor very daring; you've got no reason to feel at all proud of such an escapade. You've told lies, caused a lot of people a lot of stress, wasted a lot of time, and subjected your family to hours of worry and anxiety. You should be thoroughly ashamed of yourself. Now I'm off home. I'm absolutely fed up with the whole business. Make sure you come to school in a very different state of mind on Monday. And I want no boasting about your exploits to the other kids either. Truancy is an infection we do not want catching on in our school."

Tom's entire personality withered under this attack. With his cheeks burning he could only mumble. "Yes sir. I'm so sorry sir," as Mr Nicholls left him to the wrath of his father. But soon it was clear that Old Nick's bark had been worse than his bite. The row Tom had been sure would burst out of Dad was held at bay, after an initial flare.

"Truanting, eh! A boy of mine, truanting! I can tell you, my dad would have had the strap to me for that!"

Then, with an obvious and painful effort to tie up the anger which showed all over his face, he took a deep breath.

"And that's what I would like to do to you, but for that leg of yours, and Mr Nicholls saying you've been having a hard time and asking us not to be too tough on you. So I won't go on about the hard time you've been giving us lately. You can take yourself off to bed for the rest of the evening and we'll say no more about it. Go on, up you go."

Tom got out and up the stairs as fast as his broken leg could carry him. They all felt he was truly sorry, so meek and subdued was his manner. What no one knew was that his mood was far more affected by the disturbing nature of the afternoon's discoveries than by any remorse he felt for his actions.

Gran sneaked up later with a plate of sandwiches and a mug of tea for him.

"You're a lucky young man," she said to him as she put the plate down, trying to make her kind soft face into a stern one. "That teacher of yours said you'd been punished enough and asked Dad not to beat you. He might have done, you know."

"I know, Gran," Tom said wearily. Even Gran, his ally and supporter, Gran, who always stuck up for him, even Gran couldn't help him now.

'You're right, I have been punished enough,' he thought to himself, 'though not in any way that you could understand.'

When she had gone, he nibbled spiritlessly at a sandwich while his mind agitated around his problems. What on earth was going to happen next?

'Think about it tomorrow. Sleep on it,' his inner self told him.

But he couldn't go to sleep, for fear of still more frightening dreams taking over his head. He tried to divert himself by reading one of his favourite books, but page after page slipped under his eyes without making any sense at all. Then he started to fiddle about with the game Julie had given him. His head began to swim and his ears to ring with clinical bleeps and squeaks as the tiny figures jerked and jolted across the little screen, but no distraction could give him peace of mind. How much longer was it all going to go on? He seemed to have spent most of the last few weeks in this state of mental turmoil, agonising, protesting, questioning. With a groan he flung the game away. He must be going crazy.

"You OK, Tom?" Julie stood in the doorway. "I heard you. D'you want anything? Is it your leg? Shall I get Mum, or what?"

Tom had almost forgotten about his leg. He looked at Julie. She was over two years older than him, and when he was little, she had often provided kindly support and protection if he needed it. It was only in the last year that they hadn't got on so well. In his present mood of desperation and worry she seemed like a possible saviour.

"Julie, d'you believe in ghosts?"

"WHAT? What on earth are you talking about?"

She came further into the room, a little startled, but curious.

"Promise you won't laugh?"

"Course I won't. Go on, Tom, tell me. What's the matter?"

So he plunged straight in.

"Well, you see, it all started when I went tobogganing with Ian and Michael before Christmas. No — no — before that, even. D'you remember that day Gran told us about the church, and the flood, and the curse?"

He told her the whole story, the entire sequence of events, from the crying children he had heard the night of the blizzard, to the chilling account he had read that afternoon in Brighton in the ghost story book.

Julie didn't once ask him if he was making it up, or if he had been imagining things. She wasn't so much like a grown-up, after all. When he had finished, she stared at him, shocked, her hand over her mouth.

"Gosh, Tom, how awful! You poor thing — so scary!"

"I know."

There was a moment's silence. Then Julie recovered herself a bit.

"Perhaps you've got to break the curse or something. Maybe we're descended from the family of one of the kids who was drowned. What time of year was it? Is it the anniversary or anything like that? Oh, Tom, perhaps it's going to happen again!"

They gazed in horror at one another. As soon as Julie had said it Tom knew she was right. Why else was he being haunted by those events which had happened so long ago?

"And perhaps I'm meant to stop it happening," he said slowly. "But that's crazy. How on earth can I stop a flood? Or save people from drowning?"

"Look, Tom, maybe it isn't really like that at all. Maybe there's just something we've got to do, you know, to break the curse, like I said. But we can't do anything at all till we find out more about it. Can I have a look at the book?"

"It's in my school bag".

After reading the fateful account of the ghostly children, Tom, horrified and scared, had pushed the book back into the paper bag the bookseller had put it in, bundling it right down into the bottom of his school rucksack. While fervently wishing he had never seen it, he had known somehow that he had to hang on to it, because what he had read was not going to go away even if he got rid of the book.

He felt a little shiver of superstitious dread as Julie picked up the rucksack from the floor where he had dumped it. Amazingly, she seemed to be recovering fast from her initial shock, and ideas began to crowd into her head. She got the book out and opened it — page 193, Tom told her — and she started to scrutinise it while he waited, fearful and silent.

"I know," she was saying as she slid her eyes over the account in the book, "I know what we'll do. We must find where the book's from, you know, the history of Fulhurst Abbey one, and get the full story. Maybe this Matthias Bysouth bloke knew why there was a curse in the first place, and what all of this has to do with flooding and drowning children."

Tom started to feel as if something suffocating was being lifted away from him. Julie's acceptance of the situation and her down-to-earth suggestions for tackling it gave him new strength.

"Yeah — yeah — I s'pose we could. What a good idea! D'you think Brighton library, or p'raps Sussex University—"

"Lewes!" Julie exclaimed, shutting the book with a snap. Her secondary school was in Lewes. "Lewes library is the best place. There are loads of books about Sussex there. I know 'cos when we were doing our school Domesday project last year, we had to use some of them. And there's local archives too, at the Town Hall, and the Domesday exhibition at the museum's still on. I bet we can find something about Fulhurst Abbey!"

"Brill!"

"We'll go tomorrow. We can get the morning bus and maybe Mum will let us take a packed lunch so we have longer, if I say I'll keep you out of trouble."

Normally Tom would have protested at this, but he felt so grateful to Julie for taking on such a large share of his burden that he let it pass. Anyway, he knew that there was some truth in what she said. They would never allow him to go to Lewes on his own, especially with his leg in plaster and after today's escapade. His heart dropped again as he remembered why he was where he was.

"Jules, what if they say I can't come? 'Cos of bunking off, and all that. Dad probably won't let me."

Julie thought for a moment.

"Look, I'll find some way of persuading them. And now I'd better go back downstairs. Dad'll be mad if he thinks I'm talking to you when you're supposed to be in disgrace, and anyway, I need to finish my homework and then there's something I want to watch on telly. But try not to worry. We'll sort it, somehow."

CHAPTER 11

A Visit to the Library

The next morning Tom woke up feeling as if everything was different. Quite a lot of things were. Sharing his strange secret with Julie had made it seem more like an adventure and less like a nightmare which he and he alone was trapped inside.

He got out of bed and tested his weight on his lame leg. It felt stronger too; he tried a turn or two around his bedroom with only one crutch and decided he didn't need two any more. Even the air felt different. Mum said it was because there was a thaw coming, but to Tom it didn't seem any less cold, just different.

A whispered conversation with Julie before they went down to breakfast laid their plan for tackling their parents.

It worked. Julie set the scene by coming into the kitchen for breakfast wearing a closed, cross expression all over her face. The family knew this expression of Julie's well. Everything drooped; her mouth, her eyelids, her straight unbrushed hair hanging lankly down instead of being held back with coloured clips. It meant that she was in a very bad mood.

"What's wrong with you this morning?" Dad asked mildly.

He himself felt pretty cheerful. The weather forecast had said there was a thaw on the way, which meant soon he might get into the garden again.

"It's not fair," Julie growled, flinging herself onto her chair and grabbing a piece of toast. "I've got to spend the whole morning in Lewes library, of all places, looking up stuff about history. And there's loads of things I want to do today. It's really unfair."

"Rather you than me," Tom put in smugly. "You wouldn't catch me wasting a Saturday morning, working."

As they had calculated, this immediately got Dad going.

"Oh, wouldn't we?" he said balefully. "I'm not so sure about that, young man. I've got plenty of jobs you can do."

"Yeah, Dad," Julie continued over Tom's cry of "Oh no!"

"It isn't fair at all. Why should I spend the day doing schoolwork. It wasn't me who bunked off school yesterday. He should have to do it, not me."

Mum, trying to calm things down a bit, unknowingly played right into the children's hands.

"I'd love to have time to spend a morning at the library," she said, adding as she turned to Gran, "Wouldn't you, Mum? I can't think how long it is since I read a good book!"

"That's right dear," Gran agreed. She then had the brainwave Tom and Julie had hoped someone would have, though they had thought it would be Dad.

"I'll tell you what, why doesn't our Tom go in with Julie, then he can change his own library books and get some out for you and me, dear. We can tell him what sort of things we like; it'll be a real good deed for him to do."

"And he can also give Julie a hand looking up her bits of history," Dad added approvingly, seeing a morning of blameless and productive activity stretching out in front of his wayward son.

Tom and Julie had one more card to play.

"Oh NO, Dad!" they protested in unison.

Julie continued. "That'll make it even worse, taking him along with me. It'll take much longer too, with that bad leg of his…"

"I know what you can do," said Mum. "If Tom gets us some books and gives you a bit of help, and you get your homework done, how would you like to go and have a burger somewhere before you come home?"

"Cor, Mum, great!"

"Yeah, thanks Mum!" The delighted glances that Tom and Julie exchanged were both triumphant and grateful. Their strategy had worked perfectly.

It was hard to wait until they got out of the house before succumbing to the gales of helpless giggles which had threatened to overcome them as Mum and Gran placed their book orders with Tom: The Royal Family and showbusiness for Gran, and romances and murder mysteries for Mum. Tom wrote down their requests solemnly, not trusting himself to catch Julie's eyes. But once out of the house they let themselves go, their laughter gusting out around them in the chilly air like clouds of smoke.

"Oh, wouldn't we indeed! I'm not so sure about that, young man!" Tom said, pushing his mouth out and deepening his voice in imitation of Dad. "Well, I must say I wouldn't say no to a nice day at the library, eh Gran?"

"Ooh no dear, it's a long time since I had a good read about the Royal Family," added Julie, giggling again.

Their mirth got the better of them just as the bus arrived. Julie's voice as she bought their tickets came out strangled and strained, which set them both off again. The other passengers glanced at them, a few with irritation but most with indulgence, smiling too at such hilarity. Well-meaning remarks like "Good joke, is it?" and "Someone's really got the giggles," only made things worse. In the end what stopped them was a sort of exhaustion; by now their stomachs ached and their eyes were wet and pink with laughter. Tom couldn't remember when he had last felt so carefree.

By the time they reached the library they had got control of themselves again. The librarian was a pale, plump, slightly spotty young man with straight unshiny toffee-coloured hair and a bulging stomach incompletely confined by his trousers and jacket. Tom thought his eyes, swollen by the thick lenses of his glasses, looked like glossy boiled sweets.

"We want to find out about Fulhurst Abbey, and things round about, local history really," Julie said briskly.

"Well, the local history section's over there."

Half an hour ago the man's voice, as thin and flimsy as his body was fat and solid, would have brought back another attack of the giggles, but the moment had passed.

"There's a lot of stuff there." The librarian continued, "but you could also try the church history section in the reference library upstairs."

"Thanks."

Tom and Julie went over to the local history shelves where Tom immediately sank down onto one of the chairs which were placed at the end of each block of shelving. His leg felt achy and tired and it was bliss to get off his crutch. It was also pleasantly warm in the library after the raw chill of the streets outside.

"That's nice!" he said to himself.

Julie didn't waste any time. She started to search among the shelves, her face solemn with concentration as she scanned the rows of book titles in front of her. Every now and then she would pull one out for a closer look. If it seemed as if it might have something useful in it, she took it over to Tom, whose job it was to start looking things up in the books she had selected.

Soon they had quite a big pile, so Julie joined Tom in studying them. It was painstaking work, much more problematic than they had imagined. There was a lot of technical stuff about church architecture, full of words that neither of them understood. There was also an enormous amount of social history from the Middle Ages onwards, and they found one fascinating little volume about Sussex customs and folklore.

"Look, Tom! Customs and Folklore. I'm sure this'll have it in!"

Eagerly they pored over the book. On nearly every page there was intriguing information — about such things as Souling and Clemmening, how to make coager cakes and pond pudding, and what happened on Bending In Day. Enticing though all this was, they came to the end of the book having drawn a blank on the story they were looking for.

Tom sighed and picked up the next book. It was an uninviting looking volume called 'A History of Ten Downland Parishes in the Diocese of Lewes.' There were more than five hundred pages, each divided into two closely written columns of tiny print. Tom didn't think he could bear to look at it. What on earth was he doing spending a Saturday morning scrutinising fusty old books on church history?

A sudden yearning hit him for the uncomplicated world of the children's library, with its colourful displays of attractive looking books, its cheerful easy-going atmosphere and its red plastic chairs grouped invitingly round little tables. He stretched, a great elastic stretch which turned itself into a huge face-cracking yawn. Julie could manage on her own for a bit; he was taking a break. Besides, he had his own library books to change plus some to get for Mum and Gran, hadn't he?

"Just going to the loo, and I'll return these while I'm about it," he said casually, picking up the bag of library books.

Julie hardly looked up. She was engrossed in another book; 'The Diary of a Sussex Parson'. Feeling a bit of a traitor Tom limped over to the children's library, quelling his conscience with the resolve that he would just spend a short time looking at the Asterix and Tintin books, his favourites, then he would find out if there were any children's books on local history. After that he would go back and choose books for Mum and Gran.

It was lovely in the children's library; bright, busy and not too hushed. Last month's Christmas tree and displays of festive posters and seasonal books had been replaced by an exhibition about the Pied Piper of Hamelin. There was a frieze of rats made by local schoolchildren, a series of posters advertising a forthcoming pantomime production by the Lewes Players entitled 'The Pied Piper', and a collage made up of pictures and poetry and other information about the story.

Tom paused in front of the largest poster, which depicted the Pied Piper himself, tall and colourful in yellow and red. His head was held jubilantly high, his pipe to his lips, and his long legs striding forward with confidence and determination. Behind him, between rows of uneven roofed houses, huddled together and diminishing to nothing in the distance, stretched out a throng of children as far as the eye could see. Tom was on the point of moving on but something about the poster halted him. A lone piper, a crowd of children, a village street — all of these were images from his dreams.

What was the story of the Pied Piper? Could it have anything to do with his own mystery? Slowly Tom moved from one end of the display to the other, reading the long story-poem which was written out along the base of the collage. It didn't seem to have much relevance to Fulhurst, this tale of a plague of rats in a medieval German town, and the disappearance not just of the rats but of all the children too except for one lame boy. But Tom couldn't get out of his head the feeling that there might be some sort of message there for him.

At the end of the display was another heading — 'The Children's Crusade and the Black Death — the Truth behind the Legend?' Tom read on. It was a fascinating but tragic story. In the Middle Ages hundreds of children from all over France and Germany had left their homes and families to follow a twelve-year-old boy who said he had received messages from God. Their destination was the Holy Land, where they were going to fight in the Crusades. Some accounts said the children were all drowned at sea, some said they had been sold into slavery by pirates, and some said they had all perished in the Black Death, a deadly pandemic which was raging through Europe at the time, over seven hundred years ago.

The last of these seemed a likely enough explanation for the rats in Hamelin Town. They could have brought the plague with them; it was thought to be carried by the fleas which lived on rats, Tom learnt. Everyone who lived in the town could have died; was the little lame boy the only child left? Tom, thinking of his own lameness, felt a sort of fellow feeling with this lonely survivor.

Or could the real Pied Piper have been the boy in the Children's Crusade, Tom wondered? And if French and

German children left home to follow him, so also perhaps did some English children, maybe some of them from Fulhurst village. Could this be the origin of the ghostly children of Fulhurst? Had they all drowned at sea, on their way to join the French children? A disaster like that would surely not have been forgotten for years and years, the memory of it might have been handed down from generation to generation.

Then, long after the Abbey was closed and there was talk of a curse and a flood, maybe people recalled the old story of the disappearance and drowning of the children, and the two stories became mixed up. Tom nodded to himself. It was possible, it really was. If it was true, not only would it help to explain his nightmares of floods and curses and lost children, but it would also make them seem somehow less frightening and more logical. After all, if a story like the Pied Piper of Hamelin could grow out of such happenings, so surely could the story of the Fulhurst curse.

"There you are! I've been looking for you all over the place! I've found it, the story! Come back and I'll show you. It's in two books, come ON, Tom!"

Julie was flushed and triumphant, and so excited she couldn't speak coherently.

"It's the same bloke, the one who wrote the book about the Abbey, Matthias Bysouth. There's his diary — he was Rector of Fulhurst, and he was there for the flood that Gran told us about. And he talks about the Man in Black, so it isn't just your imagination, it's real, Tom. Oh, come back to the adult library quick, Tom, let me show you!"

97

Tom had been so lost in his own thoughts that it took a bit of time to tune in to what Julie was saying. He wanted to pour out his own ideas, but he realised that his sister was far too worked up to concentrate on new theories. Obediently he followed her back into the adult library to see what she had discovered.

CHAPTER 12

The Fulhurst Curse

Julie led Tom over to a table in the upper storey of the adult library, where the reference books were kept. There were a few young people working there, heads bent over solid looking textbooks and paper spread over the tables in front of them, but most of the chairs were occupied by older people reading newspapers. Tom noticed one old man who had fallen asleep over his copy of the Daily Express; his head kept drooping slowly down then jerking suddenly up again. A transparent thread of saliva hung down from the corner of his open mouth and lay in a grey smudge on the newspaper. Tom stared for a few moments, then looked away, embarrassed.

"I moved over here 'cos there's more room," Julie said. "And it's where I found this other book, the big one here."

She pointed to a heavy volume bound in faded green leather which lay open on the table. It gave off a slightly stale, musty smell, as if it hadn't been opened for years. Tom looked at the spine of the book, on which were imprinted the words 'A History of the Abbey of Fulhurst'. He flipped open the cover.

"That's the book they told about in 'Sussex Ghost Stories'," he said.

"Yes it is — but first, Tom, look at this one, it's Matthias Bysouth's diary. Just read the bits here, about the flood."

The diary was much smaller, a thin book with a mottled red cover. Dutifully Tom hung his crutch on a chair and slipping into the one next to it he began to read. He couldn't understand it all; the language was old-fashioned and there were quite a lot of unfamiliar words. But he could grasp enough to be drawn into the drama of those few terrible days more than one hundred years ago:

'February 18th, 1876. So tired I can hardly write. An appalling catastrophe came to Fulhurst today. After all the rain of this past week the river could no longer contain itself. With a crash like the coming of the Apocalypse it burst through its bank and drowned the lower end of the village. My poor church is in a sorry state, the furnishings ruined, the carpeting and the hassocks waterlogged, the books and chairs floating in two feet of water. But this is nothing compared to the human tragedy. The church was empty, thank heaven, but the entire lower part of the village has suffered terribly. Most of the cottagers managed to flee to safety, but their possessions are destroyed — how much more poverty-stricken their lives will be now. We had to rescue some of those from Ful-End

Cottages through their upper windows. Worst of all, there are a few missing still.

February 20th, 1876. The flood is abating but the scene is one of desolation such as I never thought to see. There is mud everywhere; broken windows, pieces of furniture, books, clothing and household equipment lie strewn over the ground, anchored in the mud — the flotsam and jetsam of our stricken community. We recovered the bodies of poor Henry and Kate Leigh today, and that of Granny Crocker. I can at least thank God that this time no children were lost. Perhaps the ancient curse is losing its strength. I am certain that no one has reported seeing the dark monk during this disaster, a matter of some relief to me, for there is enough to do here without coping with that sort of alarm and superstition. Was the drowned boy about forty years ago perhaps the last hostage to that old story? I hope and pray so. Our poor community needs help and hope to rebuild its present and to face its future, not to be haunted by the fatalities of the past.'

Tom came to the end of the entry for the 20th of February and turned the page with a combined feeling of fear and hope. Would there be any more about the dark monk — who was surely the same apparition as his Man in Black? But the rector had apparently not had time to write in his diary again for several weeks. The next entry was for mid-March and was dedicated to the setting up of a disaster fund to repair flood damage and help the stricken villagers.

"There's quite a lot I don't get, for instance that drowned boy. What's that about? I thought there were lots of drowned children — and anyway, it all happened long before that, the Sussex Ghost Story book said — in sixteen something. Forty years before 1876 would only be 1836."

Julie pushed the other much larger and heavier book over, Matthias Bysouth's 'A History of the Abbey of Fulhurst'.

"I know, but now you've got to read this."

It was a much harder thing to tackle than the diary. The print was tiny and cramped, the pages thin and yellowed, and it was full of long words and difficult sentences. But contained in those uninviting looking pages, carefully chronicled by the bygone rector, was the tragic background to Tom's unearthly visitations. With Julie's help he made his way through the close-written pages laying bare the whole terrible story.

It had all happened more than three hundred years before Matthias Bysouth became Rector of Fulhurst, and four hundred and fifty years before Tom himself had started seeing and hearing ghosts.

In 1536 Fulhurst Abbey was flourishing. It was the spiritual home and workplace for seventy Benedictine monks and twenty-five young boys who were novices training for the priesthood. Around the Abbey were fields and orchards where the monks harvested fruit and grain. They had a large kitchen garden where they grew vegetables and herbs; the herbs were used not only to spread on the floors of the Abbey and its surrounding buildings, but also to create a variety of medicines and ointments to help the monks in their care of the sick. From the fleeces of their sheep, which they herded on the hills around the Abbey, they made woollen cloth for their own black vestments and to sell so they could enrich the foundation further. Each day passed peacefully and busily, divided, as the days had been for centuries, into periods for prayer, for work and for worship.

The Abbey was rich, despite the simple hardworking lifestyle of the monks. As well as its fertile land and gardens there were plenty of treasures inside. The library was famous for its many fine books and illuminated manuscripts, and in the Abbey's Great Church were kept silver cups, gold and jewelled crucifixes and beautiful paintings. Over the high altar was a huge medieval fresco of Judgement Day; the souls of the damned disappearing into a deep pit while the spirits of the virtuous ascended into the gold and blue heavens, wafted on their way by angels. The chapels on both sides of the nave and aisles were also richly decorated with frescoes depicting events from the Bible.

On the throne at the time was King Henry VIII, who had serious financial problems. His extravagant lifestyle had left very little money in the royal treasury. Another problem was that a few years earlier he had quarrelled with the Pope, who had refused to annul his marriage to Queen Katherine so he could marry his mistress Anne Boleyn. This part of the story was familiar to Tom; they had been learning about the Tudors at school last term.

By 1534 Henry had married Anne, he then split from the Pope and made himself Head of the Church. Short of money, within the next two years the King now decided that he was entitled to a share of the riches of the monasteries. This was the backdrop to the fate of Fulhurst Abbey and many other religious foundations all over the land.

Fulhurst Abbey was to be emptied and the monks dismissed, and the whole estate would now belong to the Crown. Obviously, the monks of Fulhurst were bitterly opposed to this takeover. At first, few of them believed it would really happen; surely God would save them. They carried on just as they had always done, the centuries-old rituals and duties continuing to fill their days.

One day in the summer of 1536 an armed company of the Kings Men arrived and seized a great many of the treasures of the Abbey. The monks were horrified and frightened. Some of them said they would serve the King in the new Church of England, some disappeared into the villages and towns round about and were never heard of again, but most fled to France, taking the remainder of the Abbey's treasures with them.

One monk refused to leave. He was Brother Nicodemus, who had been in charge of the seminary for young boys training for the priesthood. Some of those boys had left when the monks did, returning to their families or crossing the channel with the fugitive monks to join French monasteries. But about half of them stayed behind; Brother Nicodemus must have been much loved by them to inspire such loyalty. He seemed to have been a man of very strong character, with a magnetic and commanding personality. There was something about his leadership which made those boys willing to put up with the hardships and dangers of their changed lives in the deserted Abbey.

It was a strange new life. They were now outlaws, so Brother Nicodemus had to organise raiding parties on the estates which had been seized. The Abbey's sheep, like its land, were now Crown property, and the Abbey's treasures all gone, so Brother Nicodemus and the boys had to scavenge and steal food to survive. As the year edged round things got worse. The days were cold and the nights long. Their stores of grain were nearly finished, there was nothing left growing in the gardens, and they were having to chop up and burn some of the heavy oak furniture in the Abbey buildings to keep warm.

Another of the boys slipped away, unable to stand such a hard life. But to most of those left, the Abbey was the only home they had ever known. They believed every word Brother Nicodemus said when he told them what a wicked, godless place the outside world was. If they stayed, working and praying under his guidance, God would protect them. But Brother Nicodemus was to be proved catastrophically wrong.

The fateful day was January 6th, 1537. The weather was bitterly cold. Life for the beleaguered community at the Abbey could hardly have been worse. There was no food, hardly any firewood, and little hope of replenishing supplies, for the hilltop villages around were full of soldiers, stationed up there to keep watch on the coast in case of French aggression.

The date was Twelfth Night, the religious feast of the Epiphany, and Brother Nicodemus was determined that they would celebrate the festival. They had managed to eat meat at Christmas — a pair of lambs which had strayed together into the Abbey grounds. They had been sent by God, Brother Nicodemus said, offering up prayers of thanksgiving. But there was no repeat of such good fortune at Epiphany.

Brother Nicodemus told the boys to stay in the Lady Chapel and practice their hymns and chants for the Epiphany service, while he himself went out to scavenge for the feast. Somehow, he managed to avoid the soldiers and a few hours later he made his way back to the Abbey with a couple of chickens over one shoulder and a sack of barley over the other. But as he turned towards home a terrible sight met his eyes.

The Abbey and its surrounding buildings were on fire. Gusts of grey smoke flapped round the great tower like a shroud. Through the pointed windows he could see molten yellow and orange spikes of flame leaping greedily up inside. The huge, decorated rose window at the end of the nave had buckled and crashed to the ground, a million fragments of coloured glass. And the Lady Chapel where he had left the boys was a blackened ruin.

Brother Nicodemus let out a loud cry and rushed over to one of the small knots of people who stood silently on the hillside, huddled together, watching. He grabbed a man by the shoulders.

"Where are the children?"

The man jerked his thumb towards the charred wreck of the chapel.

"They wouldn't come out, they just kept on singing."

Brother Nicodemus pushed the man violently away from him. He began to scream curses at them all in a voice so distorted by grief and passion that it sounded hardly human.

"I curse you all!" he cried. "For hundreds of years you will be cursed; on the fifty years I have lived I curse you thrice, in the name of the Father, in the name of the Son, in the name of the Holy Ghost. By fire and air, you have destroyed us; by earth and water shall be destroyed your children, and your children's children!"

With the echoes of his voice still bouncing back from the hills around he dashed straight through the blazing doorway into the flame-filled church.

By the time Tom reached the end of this horrifying account his vivid imagination was working overtime. He imagined hearing the screams of the doomed boys as they burnt to death in the chapel. In his head was an image of the Abbey in flames. Like another shot from the same imaginary film came another picture — the faces of those watching. Tom had once seen a warehouse on fire in Brighton. All around there had been crowds of people, their faces lit up by the glow of the flames, staring in mingled shock and fascination. They were held on the spot by the drama of what was happening, unable to tear themselves away. It must have been like that when the Abbey burned. He shuddered and closed the book, the last frenzied words of Brother Nicodemus seeming to ring in his ears.

"Oh my God, Julie, what an awful thing!" He felt shocked and shaky.

Julie was sitting opposite him, her elbows on the table and her chin in her hands.

"I know. And that isn't all. There must be more, later. Somewhere it has to talk about all the drowned children, you know, the ones in your Sussex Ghosts book."

"I don't know if I want to read any more."

The trouble was, neither of them could think about anything else. They had to go on searching. Together they scrutinised the book again. It wasn't easy to find what they wanted, because there was no index, but they knew the evidence must be there somewhere, because the book Tom had bought in Brighton had quoted it.

"1687, that's when it was," Julie remembered. "Let's see what was happening in 1687."

In the end they did find it. There wasn't much more detail than there had been in Tom's book; but Matthias Bysouth went on to try to explain the incident. The dark monk, he said, could have been the ghost of Brother Nicodemus, and the river bursting its banks, flooding the church and drowning the children could have been the fulfilment of the curse by earth and water. As a caution he added that it was probably all superstition and folklore and should not be taken too seriously.

Julie and Tom didn't agree. They were taking it extremely seriously.

"It's — sort of — as if he took those children to replace his own boys," Tom suggested, trying to understand.

Julie nodded, frowning.

"You mean the ghosts those people saw, the ghosts of those children going up the hill?"

"Yes, he was taking them away to the old Abbey. Oh Julie, it's all really creepy but it's also so sad!"

Julie was considering the timings.

"But I'll tell you what the creepiest thing of all is, Tom. That it's still going on. Have you noticed the dates of all these things? 1537. The Abbey was burnt. 1687, the children were drowned. About forty years before 1876 — say 1837, another boy was drowned. And what year are we in now?"

"1987." Tom began to see a pattern emerging.

Julie, one step ahead of him, went on, thinking aloud.

" Listen, Tom, I think I see it now, it's every, er, not a hundred, but every hundred and fifty years. Brother Nicodemus's fifty years — fifty for the Father, fifty for the Son, and fifty for the Holy Ghost. Three times fifty makes a hundred and fifty. That's what he meant!"

"But what about 1876? And the other floods, before and after Brother Nicodemus's time?"

"Well," Julie said, "Yes, there have been other floods, both before and after, as you say. But we know that the river does flood often 'cos it's so low down, so some of them would probably have happened anyway, the 1876 one could just have been one of those. And no children were lost that time."

"But this year now — because of the date — and because of all the scary things that have been going on — must mean that something awful, to do with the old curse, really is going to happen." Tom's voice was panicky. He felt horribly shocked and frightened about the significance of what they had discovered.

"Unless we can do something to stop it. We *have* to be able to, Tom, otherwise why would all those strange things have happened to you, it must be a sort of warning. You know that's what you've been feeling all this time. Now at least we know what it's all about, so we can — oh I don't know, make plans, warn people — something must be possible."

"I suppose so." Tom sounded scared and doubtful. What on earth could they do? And who on earth would believe them if they did warn anyone? They were just a couple of kids.

Julie got up, impatient and eager.

"Come on, let's get Mum's and Gran's books and go and have something to eat. Then we can make some plans."

Yet again Tom was amazed by his sister. She seemed to be so much less affected than he by the horrors of it all. It was a dreadfully daunting thing to have to face up to, but here she was, all ready to leap forward, full of optimism and courage.

"OK, I'm coming." Food was definitely a good idea.

But it wasn't until they had finished their burgers and chips and felt pleasantly full and therefore rather more optimistic, that Tom thought of something.

"Julie!"

"Yes."

"They keep talking about Epiphany, Twelfth Night, you know. The Abbey burnt down on Epiphany, and the 1687 children were in church singing in a Twelfth Night service. Well, Twelfth Night is January the 6th, and that was last Tuesday. We sang the Epiphany Anthem last Sunday. And nothing has happened."

Did this mean that the curse was losing its power and that there wasn't anything to worry about any more? Tom pointed out too that in the last incident, the 1837 one, only one boy had drowned. Had Tom's meetings with the Man in Black, Brother Nicodemus, the dark monk, been the beginning and the end of it? Was the danger fading away? On the other hand, perhaps the actual day wasn't so important, and they were still in the danger period.

"It still counts as Epiphany in the church calendar right up until the start of Lent six weeks later," Tom said. Being in the church choir meant he knew about such things.

"Oh great!" exclaimed Julie, "So we have to be on the alert to save kids from drowning for the next six weeks?"

They spent the bus ride home discussing it. They agreed that it probably wasn't all over, but maybe the danger might be getting less acute. It was Julie's friend

Christina however, who unknowingly showed them why the peril was yet to come, although the 6th of January had passed.

CHAPTER 13

Christina's Evidence

The next day Tom didn't have to go to church. The choir were having a week off after all their efforts over the Christmas season. He woke up with a wonderful, light-hearted feeling. The day lay ahead of him, empty and free as Sundays rarely were.

At breakfast Dad made a surprise announcement.

"We're all going to Eastbourne. I've got tickets for the Christmas panto there; Aladdin, it is. I was going to tell you on Friday, but it didn't seem the right time, one way and another."

He glanced over, with a half-smile, at Tom, who grinned sheepishly, remembering Friday.

"Anyway, we'll get over there and have our dinner before the show. So, get your beds made, kids, and spruce yourselves up a bit. I'll give the car a wash and then we'll get a move on."

Julie and Tom exchanged delighted glances and promptly let their secret concerns drop into the basements of their brains. So Sunday raced by gaily as if the Man in Black had never been.

It wasn't until two days later, when Julie brought her friend Christina home from school with her to spend the evening and stay the night, that the Fulhurst curse forced its way into the forefront of Tom's mind again.

Christina was Julie's best friend. She lived in Lewes where her parents had a shop and café. Although to talk to she sounded just as much a native of Sussex as Tom and Julie, her light brown skin, dark brown eyes and thick black hair were clues to a more unusual origin. Christina came from a Greek Cypriot family.

Her parents had emigrated to England in the early 1970's, when unstable politics between the Turks and the Greeks on the island had led to a state of civil war. Christina had been born in England soon after they arrived, but her elder brother Giorgios was four years old when they left Cyprus, and he sometimes talked about how frightened he had been by the fighting in the streets.

Christina's parents, with their accented English and the foreign-feeling atmosphere of their home and shop, seemed exotic and glamorous to Julie. She loved visiting the family, eating strange but delicious food and listening in admiration as Christina switched from speaking English into Greek and back again.

To Tom, Christina was no different from Julie's other friends, giggly and annoying and secretive. Before school that morning he had waylaid Julie.

114

"You won't tell Christina anything, will you? About you know what, I mean."

Julie was in a teasing mood.

"I might, I might not!"

"JULIE! Oh please."

"OK, OK. But there's no need for you to fuss just because my friend's coming over. I don't have to spend all my time mucking about with little boys, you know. I hope you're going to leave us alone while Chris is here, we won't want you hanging around."

Julie had been such an ally lately that Tom had forgotten how different she became when she had a friend over.

"You must be joking," he retorted, barging past her with his crutch as they left for school — she to wait for her bus and he to continue his limping progress along the street to his school.

He soon decided, though, that there was no point in falling out with her; so he called out cheerfully.

"Bye Jules, see you later," as she got on the school bus. The last thing he wanted was to lose his sister's support in dealing with their shared dark secret.

At teatime that evening he made every effort to be friendly and cheerful. One thing he really enjoyed about Christina's visits was that she always brought some sweets or cakes from the shop to share for tea. They were often unusual and slightly exotic things, sweet crunchy nutty halva, rose flavoured Turkish Delight, or a string of almonds wrapped round with chewy grape jelly. This time it was a cake.

"It's a Greek New Year cake," Christina explained. "You have to give all your relations a slice and cut a slice for St Basil too. In one slice there's a piece of money. Whoever gets it has good luck for the whole of the next year."

"A bit like Christmas pudding, isn't it," said Gran, getting a sharp knife and handing it to Christina to cut the cake.

"What happens if the money's in St Basil's slice," asked Tom.

Christina started cutting slices of the cake and passing them round the table.

"Then the whole family will have good luck. But I don't think there's real money in these bought ones. My Dad gets them from a wholesaler."

She was right, but Julie was nonetheless delighted when something tinkled onto her plate, and she picked up a little metal charm in the shape of a bell.

"What a delicious cake!" Mum said, scooping up the last few crumbs from her plate. "Nuts and orange I can taste, and some spicy stuff. But what are these seeds on top, Chris?"

"Sesame seeds. We use them a lot — we also have them on the buns we eat at Easter. My Yaya — my granny — makes brilliant Easter buns, and whenever we can we go back to Cyprus to spend Easter with her. But this year it's going to be too late. We can't miss school, so Yaya will send us a box of her buns and we'll celebrate Easter here."

Tom didn't understand.

"But Easter's always in the Easter holidays, you wouldn't ever miss school for it."

"It often isn't, for us. The Greek Easter's nearly always later, 'cos the Greek Orthodox Church still uses the old calendar for Easter."

"What d'you mean, the old calendar?" All at once Julie was alert. She glanced quickly at Tom, but he still looked baffled.

"Well, I'm not really sure. But all I know is that everything's one or two weeks later than in the normal calendar. Some bits of the Orthodox Church still have Christmas later too, but we just do Easter and Pentecost. I think it used to be the whole year round, though, in the olden days."

By now Tom too had woken up to the significance of what Christina had said.

"Was it in England as well in the olden days?" he asked. Christina shrugged her shoulders. She wasn't really all that interested.

"I suppose so. Please may me and Julie leave the table, Mrs Lulham?"

It was Tom's turn to help with the washing up. He bent over the sink, his hands submerged in the warm frothy water, and shifted the dishes about, but his mind wasn't on what he was doing. If the old calendar Chris had mentioned had been in use in England, everything must have been up to two weeks later then, including Epiphany. And that would mean that it wouldn't have happened yet.

117

Ghosts and curses wouldn't suddenly change their routines because the calendar had changed, would they? So old Epiphany must be the fateful day when the curse would be fulfilled again. Somehow, he must find out if this was right. Who on earth did he know who could tell him about the old calendar?

"Come on, Tom, you're just playing with those dishes. We'll be here all night clearing up at this rate." His mother, tea towel in hand, interrupted his thoughts.

"Sorry Mum." For a few moments Tom washed dishes rapidly, his mind working just as furiously. Then he had an idea.

"Mum?"

"Yes, lovey?"

"When I've done this, d'you think I could ring Mike up? It's over a week since they moved, and I do miss him. Specially with Julie having a friend over to play."

How could Mum refuse such a wistful appeal? She couldn't.

"Of course, you can, dear. And give them all the best from us. Their new number's in the little book on the table by the phone."

It was lovely to talk to Michael again. He had started in the top class of a large primary school in Crawley, about four times the size of Fulhurst village school. The children were nice, and he had made a few friends already, but he missed Ian and Tom.

"It's fun living in a town though. There's a cinema just down the road and a wicked toyshop round the corner!

Mum says you can come and stay for a weekend soon when your leg's better perhaps."

"Yeah man! Great! Can't wait!"

But Tom couldn't forget the real purpose of his call, so after a few more minutes chatting he asked Mike if he could speak to his father. Without actually telling a lie he managed to give the impression that he needed the vicar's help with something he was doing at school.

"Hello Tom, nice to hear from you," came the vicar's familiar voice down the line. "How's the leg? And how can I help?"

"Getting a bit better, thanks Mr Cooke. Sorry to bother you but I need to find out about the old calendar, the one that was used in the olden days."

"The old calendar — do you mean the Julian calendar?"

"Is that the one the Greek Orthodox use?"

"Yes indeed, and so did we in this country until about the middle of the eighteenth century," said the vicar. "Now what exactly do you need to know, because it's rather complicated."

"Well, why did it get changed, really. What difference does it make?"

"OK. You see, Tom, the trouble with the old calendar was that over hundreds and hundreds of years, tiny errors had built up because according to the sun there are a bit more than three hundred and sixty-five days in the year. So all the extra bits of time mounted up till they made quite a big time-lag, which meant that the spring equinox — that's the day when night and day are the same length — was getting too far away from Easter. With me so far?"

"Sort of. But why does it need to be near Easter?"

"Oh well, traditionally the way we calculate the date of Easter is based on the first full moon after the spring equinox. There used to be a pagan spring festival round about then, long before Christian times, you see, so the old festival and the new were thrown together by the early Christian church. Anyway, going back to the calendar, the time came when the astronomers had to work out a more accurate calendar so those extra bits of time wouldn't mount up so much again. That was the Gregorian calendar, which we use now, and which was gradually adopted nearly everywhere. Those extra bits of time are why we have Leap Years — an extra day in February nearly every four years to mop up the leftover time."

The vicar was right, it was complicated. "But what about the Orthodox Church." Tom persisted.

"The Orthodox Church decided to stick to the old calendar for some of its religious festivals including Easter, because their priests said that Easter should always take place after the Jewish Passover. Since that's nearly always a bit after our Easter, the Orthodox Easter is still later."

"Oh, I think I get it now."

The vicar went on, "I'm afraid it's all rather confusing, Tom. But the really important thing to remember is that although we don't exactly know when our Lord rose from the grave, we do know that it was in spring. So, all Christians celebrate it with a spring festival, some a bit later than others."

Tom wasn't all that interested in the religious aspect, but he had one more question about the calendar.

"So, before they stopped using the old calendar, was Christmas really in January, if you know what I mean?"

"It was indeed, by today's reckoning. The Julian calendar's January started later than ours does today. The difference gets a tiny bit more every year, but it's roughly two weeks later, between twelve and fourteen days I think this year; maybe a bit less."

"Thanks ever so much, Mr Cooke, that's really helpful. But I'd better stop now. Mum and Dad send best wishes."

As soon as he had fended off the vicar's polite enquiries as to the welfare of his family, Tom started to work out dates. Next Tuesday was January 20th, exactly two weeks after Twelfth Night. That day, or perhaps one of the two days immediately before it, would be the fateful day — Epiphany old style, exactly four hundred and fifty years after Brother Nicodemus's horrific curse. That meant that at the most he and Julie only had six days to find out what disaster might be threatening the children in the village and how they could prevent it.

Tom hung about outside Julie's bedroom for a bit. The door was firmly closed, blank and hostile. He could hear bursts of laughter and music playing within, but he knew it was no good. Julie was out of bounds to him until Christina was gone. With an effort he resisted the temptation to kick the door with his good foot and returned downstairs. There he tried to numb his mind with television until bedtime. Tomorrow would have to do.

CHAPTER 14

Andrew Peck

School finished at lunchtime the following day. Most of the teachers were going on strike for the afternoon to join a big rally in Brighton in protest against planned changes to the primary school curriculum. Tom took little interest in the reason for the strike; people were always grumbling about the government, but everything seemed to stay more or less the same whether they grumbled or not. However, neither he nor any of the other children were indifferent to the immediate effect of the strike as far as they were concerned. As soon as school dinner was over, they flooded joyfully out of the gates.

At first Tom had intended to go straight home so that he and Julie could spend the rest of the afternoon planning what they could do to avert any possible oncoming catastrophe. Then he remembered that Julie's school wasn't going on strike, so he would have to idle away three hours or so before she got back. All that was in store for him now at home was the television to watch, the shop — with Mum and Gran always ready to use an extra pair of hands, even if the legs that went with them couldn't run any errands — and his bedroom which needed to be tidied.

If only Ian and Michael were still around, the three of them would have headed off happily to one of their hideouts, or perhaps gone up onto the downs to play. Alone, Tom was indecisive. He didn't want to go home just yet, but where should he go? What could he do?

For a short time, he joined a group of younger boys and girls who were leaning over the parapet of the bridge chucking stones and lumps of ice at the frozen skin of the river. The slight thaw of the last few days had loosened the frost's rigid grip so the ice was becoming fragile and brittle. Tom propped his crutch against the bridge and sent a large stone crashing down into the river, spreading the pointed pattern of a broken window onto the sheet of ice.

The others applauded him. "Nice one, Tom!"

"Great shot!"

If Tom had felt as carefree as they were, he would have stayed and played with them for longer, but as he stood there, the heavy weight of his hidden responsibility settled inside him. These little kids were all Fulhurst children. Could they unknowingly be under a sentence of death from the Man in Black's curse? How on earth could he possibly do anything to prevent it, if such an appalling calamity really was about to take place?

A sense of isolation more desolate and more hopeless than ever descended on him, holding him apart from his light-hearted companions. Slowly he picked up his crutch, turning away from his schoolfellows lest they should somehow read his bleak secret in the expression on his face.

"I'm off. Cheerio mates!"

Somehow Tom managed to keep his voice fairly normal as he moved away as quickly as he could. Without a backward glance, he made his way over the bridge and down the other side. There was a path which went along beside the river; it was slippery with ice and mud, uneven and bumpy underfoot. Tom had to plant his crutch carefully with each step, picking his way along painstakingly and slowly. As he continued, the shouts of those children on the bridge dropped back behind the noises in the immediate air: the steady drip of slowly melting ice and the rasping call of a rook in the trees above.

He hadn't been along this way since his ill-fated skating expedition. He shuddered. This was not only the way to the skating pond but also towards the fields where he and his friends had tobogganed, and he had first seen the Man in Black. What if he should see him again?

Tom stopped abruptly. He didn't want to go any further. He was scared suddenly, his heart jumping in his chest. Perhaps he would just go home after all. But what was that noise? Was it just a singing in his ears, or could he hear something else? Was it a ragged chorus of children's voices, thin and distant, shrilling through the still air?

"Alleluia, alleluia!"

No, surely it was nothing, it was probably children playing in the village.

124

He must be letting his imagination play tricks with him, turning those remote cries into the tune he had heard in his dream.

"I tried to save them too, you know."

Tom spun round, nearly losing his balance. There was a boy standing a little way away from him. He was about Tom's age, and rather like Tom to look at, with the same straight dark hair and bony face and sticking out ears. But his hair was longer, and his clothes looked odd, a thick grey coat and cap, a pair of baggy leather trousers, and bulky boots on his feet.

"What!" Tom was so startled he didn't take in what the boy had said.

Who was he, and where had he come from? Certainly not from Fulhurst, Tom was sure he would recognise any of the boys from the village, and some from nearby villages too. He did have some vague feeling that he might have seen the boy before, but couldn't place the memory.

"I tried to do what you're going to do. I tried to save 'em from drowning, but nothing happened. It was only me in danger that time."

"What — what are you talking about? Who are you?"

"Andrew Peck's my name. I think we're related. I hope you make a better job of it than I did. I thought I was leading the children to safety from the flood, but they weren't there. I had just had the fever, and the singing and the waters were all in my head."

For a moment Tom forgot how strange all this was. He wasn't the only one! Someone else had heard the singing and knew about the danger ahead! A glow of relief flowed over him like a beam of warm sunshine.

"I heard them singing too, just now," he said. "D'you know what's going to happen next. Are you here to help me?"

"It's up to you now. When the snow is melting fast and the river rises, you'll have to lead the children away from the flooded church to the high ground by the old Abbey. If you don't, more children may drown."

Tom's shock and bewilderment must have shown on his face because Andrew grinned reassuringly at him.

"Don't worry. I failed, but you can succeed. Just beware of the ice on the frozen pond. That was where I came to grief."

Tom looked towards the pond not far ahead of them. Its surface still seemed to be stuck fast with ice.

"Me too," he said, thinking of his own accident. "That was how this happened." He slapped his injured leg.

Andrew nodded.

"I know. But don't worry. After all, the lame boy was the only one left to face the future in Hamelin Town. You have to be like the piper who led the children away and also like the lame boy who stayed behind to give the town a future. Two people in one."

So that was the message of the Pied Piper story, was it? But how on earth did Andrew know about it? Had he also been in the library, and understood something that Tom had missed? Tom turned back to Andrew.

"So was the Pied Piper meant to be a sort of clue?"

He spoke to the air. Andrew had gone. And as Tom began to gather his thoughts together again, he remembered exactly when he had seen Andrew before. Andrew was the pipe-playing boy from his dream.

CHAPTER 15

Puzzles and Plans

"Another ghost," said Julie.

She was lying on her stomach on her bed, holding her chin in her cupped hands. Tom leaned restlessly against the wall by the door and fiddled abstractedly with a bit of Lego which he'd found in his pocket. He didn't want to agree with her, but he knew she must be right. He tried to think of another explanation, but it didn't sound very convincing, even to himself.

"Well, he could've been some new person, someone who's just come to live here, I mean. We don't know everyone from these parts. OK, OK, I know, the clothes — they were old-fashioned looking — but he was so nice, not at all scary, nothing like the Man in Black."

"So? Not all ghosts have to be scary." Julie spoke with great authority despite the fact that she'd never seen one. "I expect horrid people turn into horrid ghosts, and nice people make nice ghosts. Why should all ghosts be frightening? Honestly, Tom, what else could he have been? Those funny old clothes — who wears leather trousers these days, apart from motorcyclists? Also, that slightly fussy way of talking, a bit olden days-ish. You must be the sort of person who sees ghosts. If you can see one, why shouldn't you see more?"

Her logic was inescapable. Tom had to agree.

"OK, OK," he said again. "But who was he in real life? Why did he say we were related? And what's he got to do with it all, I wonder?"

Julie pushed her hands up through her loose straight hair, so her fingers stuck up on either side of her head.

"Peck, Peck," she said. "I wish I could remember why the name sounds sort of familiar. Could he be one of our ancestors? Perhaps he was one of the boys in the Abbey, one of those who escaped to France, who we may be descended from, so that's why you have to put it all right. Or maybe he just tried to save the kids the next time the curse happened. The children singing in the church in 1687 I mean…"

"No, no, he wasn't that old-fashioned, I'm sure," said Tom. "Wouldn't he have been wearing sort of monks' clothes if he was one of the original boys? And in 1687 I thought they wore — well, tights and doublets and things. No, he was much more — sort of — normal than that, not all that different from me." Tom sounded very certain.

In his head was a clear picture of Andrew, of his thin friendly face, his heavy coat hunched over his shoulders, its sleeves so long that Andrew's hands were almost hidden, and the cutaway skirt of the coat open at the front to reveal stained leather trousers, tied with some sort of string at the knee.

"The trouble is, we don't know when people wore clothes like that," Tom went on, thinking aloud. "But prob'ly more like a hundred years ago, I should think. Julie! Could he have been Gran's granddad, the one who was in the 1876 flood? He was only a kid when it happened, wasn't he?"

Julie shook her head. "No, 'cos actually I don't think that flood was anything to do with the curse — it was just a random sort of normal flood and nothing to do with lost children. And anyway, of course, Gran's grandad didn't die when he was a kid. But now I think about it, you're probably right about one thing — I think the boy was one of Gran's ancestors. Remember the family tree I had to make at school last year? Gran told me lots about her family history and all that. She also showed me some old photos of when she was a little girl. I'm sure that's why I recognise the name Peck, from Gran's relations."

She pulled her hands out of her hair and sat up, suddenly excited.

"I've still got that family tree somewhere; I brought it home at the end of the summer term 'cos I meant to put it on my wall, only I never did. Now, where is it? Is it in this drawer, or maybe here…" As she was talking, Julie was moving quickly about the room, opening drawers and cupboards and delving into boxes. Tom longed to help but knew she would hate him rummaging through her stuff. So he waited.

"Shall I ask Gran if we can look at her photo album?"

"Yes, good idea — but in a minute — OH! here it is! I've found it!"

It was folded up under a pile of paintings she had done at school. Eagerly they unfolded it and spread it out on the bed. The first thing they saw was the name Peck.

"Lots and lots of Pecks! I knew it was in Gran's family!" Julie exclaimed in triumph, smoothing out the chart. Tom was very intrigued.

"Look, Jules, here's Mum — Sara Woodford, and Dad — Robert Lulham — and you and me! And Aunty Ruth and Uncle Dave, and Lucy and Jane."

"But look here, Tom. This is Gran — Joan Woodford. And further up, her granddad, the one who was in the 1876 flood, John Peck, born 1868! Come on, let's work back and find all the Pecks, starting from him."

It only took a few seconds.

"Hey, look, Julie, Andrew Peck, 1826-1837. That must be him!"

"So, he was — er — Gran's granddad's dad's father's brother — his great-uncle — or he would've been if he had grown up. But what a huge family! There were nine children. Look!"

"And poor Andrew was only a kid when he died. Only eleven — just a bit older than me. Some of the others died too — Hannah Peck, in 1837 too, aged only four, and Martha Peck the same year as well — still a baby, nine weeks old. I wonder what they all died of."

"TOM!" Julie's voice was urgent. "Tom, look at the date! Andrew died in 1837. *1837*!"

Tom stared at her, his hand to his mouth.

"That was the year of the drowned boy. You don't think—"

"Of course I do. Andrew Peck must have been the drowned boy."

It all fitted. One winter day in early 1837 Andrew Peck, still feverish from the illness which had killed his little sisters, must have thought he heard or saw some children in danger. Perhaps he too had seen the Man in Black. Perhaps he had heard the old story, and had been agonising over it while still sick, possibly confusing the danger with the plight of his own little sisters. Still frail and not really in his right mind, he had set out with some idea of rescuing the children. He had trudged off alone through the snow towards the ruined Abbey, but before he reached it, he had slipped over and fallen through the thin ice of the frozen pond. Too weak to save himself, he drowned. Had he, like Tom a hundred and fifty years later, been startled by the apparition of the Man in Black and lost his footing? Unlike Tom, he hadn't survived to tell the tale. In 1837, poor Andrew Peck was the only victim of the ancient curse.

For a few moments Tom and Julie sat silently, thinking of the long dead boy. Tom was very upset. It was as if a close friend had died.

"It's horrible, horrible," he said, almost in tears. He couldn't stop picturing that mild, friendly face. Why did it have to happen to Andrew? What had he done to deserve such an awful fate? He had been so nice, so encouraging. "Oh God, Julie, I can't go on with it all. Suppose we fail too, and we get drowned as well. I'm too scared, it's all so awful."

He rolled over and lay face downwards on Julie's bed. She was as shocked as he was by all this, but less upset than poor Tom, who had actually met the boy. Patting him on the shoulder she tried to muster up some words of comfort.

"Listen, Tom, I do understand. I know it's awful, but you wouldn't feel so bad if you didn't know him. After all, lots of kids died in those days but you can't cry for them all. And the reason you do know him is 'cos he came back to help you. Which means you've been warned beforehand of the dangers, so you absolutely can't give up now, you've got to go on, for Andrew's sake as well as for all the present-day kids."

Tom didn't move. Julie sighed and stood up.

"OK, give up then. But I'll tell you what I'm going to do. I'm going to find out what's going on in the church every day till after next Tuesday. And I'm going to listen to the weather forecast every day from now on to find out if the snow's melting fast enough to cause a flood. Then I'll warn everybody what's going to happen. And no one will believe me and if you don't help me, I'll have to do it all by myself and it will probably go all wrong, 'cos it isn't me that's meant to be doing this rescue anyway. So there!"

Tom sat up again,

"OK, OK, OK, I get it. I expect you're right as usual. And I wasn't crying, anyway."

Julie wisely kept her mouth shut at this last statement, turning her attention instead to thinking about possible arrangements in church for the all-important few days leading to next Tuesday. Sunday was easy.

"The main church services, I suppose, with that replacement vicar till they get a new one. There's also Sunday school; quite a lot of kids go to that. It's in the church hall though, d'you think that counts?"

Tom frowned. "Dunno really. But they do come into the church later on, for the end of the family communion, so I suppose it does. But I think it's the choir we've got to watch out for most; after all, the boys in the Abbey were singing when it burnt."

"Right. Now Monday. What about Monday?"

"Monday — Monday," Tom pondered. "Of course! Monday evening — it has to be then!" He sounded as if he knew something Julie did not.

"Why?"

"Because there's going to be the first big 'Noye's Fludde' rehearsal there at 6.30. It's on the noticeboard at school — Old Nick was on about it again today. Kids are coming from all over the place, from lots of other schools. There'll be millions of kids — well, maybe about a hundred anyway."

Since on Tuesday there was very little going on in and around the church, it did indeed seem as if Monday was to be the crucial day. But how on earth were they going to warn all these people about a possible danger? If they told the truth — about the Man in Black, the story of the ancient curse and the ghost of Andrew Peck — no one would believe them.

If they kept quiet about all the supernatural details and just focused on warning everyone that there might be a flood, the grown-ups would tell them not to frighten the little ones and would say that if there was going to be a flood Julie and Tom should leave the arrangements to them.

All of a sudden, having knowledge of the nature of the danger ahead, with all that had to be done to prevent a catastrophic repeat of the tragedies of the past, seemed to be fraught with problems. To persuade the teachers in charge of all those who would be coming to rehearse, that they must evacuate the church and lead about a hundred children away up the hill towards the ruined Abbey on a dark winter evening, seemed a hopeless prospect.

"They'll think we're crazy," said Julie gloomily. "All the same, we'll have to have a go."

Tom agreed. "P'raps we could talk to Old Nick; I s'pose he just might listen."

They left it like that. They planned that Julie would come to meet Tom after choir practice on Friday evening and the two of them would try to have a few words with Mr Nicholls then. There didn't seem to be any better way of doing it.

Julie sighed.

"And now I suppose all we can do is keep watching the weather forecast. After all, there might not even be a flood."

That talk with Mr Nicholls never happened. In the end it wasn't necessary to warn anyone about the dangers of a possible flood. It turned out that they knew already.

CHAPTER 16

Saving the Village

At Friday morning assembly in Tom's school Mrs Clarke, the headmistress, told the children that the church was not going to be used for anything at all during the next few days.

"As some of you may know, our village church has been flooded many times before in its long history. At the moment there's a danger of it happening again. We've had an awful lot of snow this winter and now that it's melting it could fill the river so full that it might overflow. And the main place where it has overflowed in the past has been the meadow at the bottom of the village where the church is. Now, there isn't any reason for panic; the snow's melting quite slowly at the moment and the river's coping with it. But for everyone's sake we think it's best not to take any unnecessary risks, so the big 'Noye's Fludde' rehearsal on Monday will now take place in Fordinglye Church. And here's Mr Nicholls to tell you about all the arrangements."

The prospect of a flood caused different reactions among the children. Some exchanged glances of excitement — dramatic events like this didn't often come their way. Others were anxious, especially those who lived in the little houses near the church. One or two of the infants began to cry, shaken and scared by this threat to their hitherto safe world. A gabble of questions rose to people's mouths ready to jump out, and a waving field of hands sprang up into the air.

"Will it come in the school?"

"My Nan lives down Ful-End, will she be flooded?"

"Can't anyone do something to stop it?"

"Will we miss school?"

"How will we get to Fordinglye for the rehearsal?"

"What will happen to the church?"

"Hang on. Hang on." Mr Nicholls held up both hands for silence.

"Right, in a minute I'll answer all your questions, but first listen carefully to what I've got to say and perhaps you'll find you don't need to ask them after all. First of all, as Mrs Clarke says, there's no need for anyone to panic. There may not be a flood at all; after all there hasn't been one for over a hundred years, and we've had a lot of wet winters during that time. Anyhow, since the last flood the riverbank has been made much stronger and higher, so really the village is safer now than it's ever been. Also, there will be people keeping an eye on things all the time over the next few days, so if the river does seem to be getting too high, we can reinforce the banks even more. In fact, I'm sure that this will be done anyway, and I expect some of your parents will join the workforce to help. It certainly won't get anywhere near the school even if the river does overflow, because up here we're on the hill on the other side of the church where it's much higher ground. So bad luck, all those of you who were hoping for an extra holiday!" At this he paused with a smile, looking over at a few disappointed faces, then went on. "Now, about 'Noye's Fludde'. We'll be contacting all the other schools involved to say that until further notice all our full rehearsals will be over at Fordinglye Church. Will anyone who thinks they'll have difficulty getting there come and see me in my classroom at playtime, so I can arrange lifts. Oh, and the same arrangements will apply to church services, Sunday School et cetera until there's no more danger. Choir practice in the church is cancelled too till all this is over. So, are there any more questions?"

"Sir! Sir! We're doin' a play about a flood an' now we might be gonna have a real flood!"

While Mr Nicholls dealt with this artless comment (by Damian Blake, an infant who was going to be one of the animals in the Ark) and all the others that followed it, Tom sat silent among the clamour of voices. Spreading all over him was a great golden glow of relief. He felt almost as if he was coming alive again. The burden of dread and fear he had carried inside himself for so long that he had forgotten what life was like without it, had suddenly evaporated and become weightless.

He no longer had to worry! The grown-ups were in charge! Their safety-net of careful plans would put a stop to the tormented activities of the Man in Black far more effectively than he, despite all he knew, could have done. Only he and Julie would ever know about the terrors of the last weeks.

So immense was Tom's sense of liberation that he couldn't stop a huge grin spreading over his face. His classmates, who had grown used to a withdrawn, rather solemn Tom since his accident and after Ian and Michael had left, were relieved to see him smiling again. Tom even had a few kind words for poor Tony Foley, who was agitated and upset because his Nan lived at Ful-End.

"Don't worry, Tone. She'll be able to stay up the village with you and your Mum. Anyway, prob'ly nothing'll happen. But everyone'll help her move her stuff, you'll see. I'll come, and I'll get my dad and Julie to help too."

Tony stared at him, quite speechless. What could possibly have happened to make Tom Lulham — *Tom Lulham*, of all people, turn so matey all of a sudden?

When school finished that day, the children could plainly see, as they headed for home, that efforts to halt the threatened flood were already underway. People had been working all afternoon around the low point of the river. This was the meadow area around the bridge, with the church on one side of the narrow road, and the cottages on the other, between the road and the river. It wasn't all that far from where Tom had had that haunting encounter with Andrew Peck, only a couple of days before.

Things were already beginning to look very different. There were heavy black fertiliser sacks, filled with soil and sand, piled up beside the bridge and along the riverbanks.

Further along, in front of the church and also between the cottages and the river, men were putting up barricades of wood. They used all sorts of things — pieces of fencing, pallets and even trestle tables from the village hall, propped up on their sides and held in place with more sandbags stacked up behind them.

"Get along now, you kids, out of the way. We need to get all this lot up before dark!" one man shouted at the loitering children. He wiped his hands down the front of his trousers then rubbed them together for a moment. It was cold work.

Tom knew he couldn't do anything to help, but he didn't want to go. It gave him a warm comfortable feeling to see all this effort going on for the protection of the village.

"Quite a business, isn't it, Tom?" said a voice behind him. It was Mr Nicholls, on his way over to the church to collect some books.

"Yeah! Is the church still open then, sir?"

"Mmm, it is for the time being, but once all the moveable stuff has been taken out it'll be locked up till the river is back to normal. That's the next thing to be done, when all the barricades are up, both here and around the cottages. With luck we'll be able to avoid too much damage to people's property even if the river does flood over."

Tom, reluctant to leave, accompanied Mr Nicholls to the vestry door.

"Why didn't they do all this the other times, I wonder — guard against the flood, I mean. They must've realised what was going to happen."

Mr Nicholls pushed the door open.

"Well, in the past people believed firmly that God protected churches even more than anywhere else. They would hide in the church for safety from danger — sanctuary, it was called. Probably they couldn't believe God would let the church be flooded. And indeed, in most cases they were right, because churches were nearly always built on higher ground. Of course, you know the story of the founding of this church, don't you?"

"Wasn't it that some bloke was beaten-up by the river, but then his life was saved by a strange traveller who turned out to be an angel, and who bathed his wounds in the river and miraculously healed them. And the man was so grateful he said he would build a church at the very spot where he had been healed."

Mr Nicholls nodded. "That's right. He had some sort of vision and was a changed character from then on."

Tom thought uneasily about his own encounters with the supernatural.

"Prob'ly wasn't a vision at all," he said, shying away from the idea of another mystic phenomenon. "Maybe the angel was the same bloke who attacked him having second thoughts!"

"Could be, Tom," Mr Nicholls said with a smile. "Anyway, it's one way of explaining why they built a church in such an inappropriate spot. And now, don't you think it's time you hopped off home?"

"OK, sir. But d'you need any help, moving things and that?"

142

"Not now thanks, and certainly no moving of furniture for you, with that bad leg. But there may well be things you could help with tomorrow. Come down in the morning. 'Bye now."

Mr Nicholls turned in through the door and Tom, buoyant and optimistic, swung off up the village street towards home. Could this, after all, be the part he was meant to play in saving the children? By helping prevent the disaster happening perhaps he would be fulfilling what he had been selected to do. He determined to spend as much of the weekend as he could making himself useful around the flood meadow.

CHAPTER 17

The Flood

It was a strange and busy weekend for the people of Fulhurst. By Saturday afternoon the flood defences were all in place, although there was still no real change in the weather. The slow, steady thaw of the last few days continued gradually to swell the river, but it was still far from reaching the danger level which could turn the threat of a flood into a reality.

The atmosphere in the village was expectant and tense, even a bit excited. No one could think or talk about anything other than the matter of the moment. It was as if ordinary life had stopped and the concerns of the rest of the world had temporarily gone far away. At any time during the day on Saturday or Sunday there would be a little crowd of people leaning on the parapet of the bridge, looking earnestly down at the water flowing below.

"Level's getting a bit high," the gloomy ones would say.

"Long way to go yet," the cheerful ones would reply comfortingly.

Not content, the pessimists would pull in their lips and shake their heads.

"It's rising too fast for my liking. Don't reckon much to them defences holding out. Trestle tables'll crumple like paper once the water gets behind 'em."

"Don't you worry," would respond the optimists. "It'll never get over the banks at this rate. You wait, all this'll turn out to be a lot of fuss about nothing."

The children of the village were enjoying every minute of the crisis; it felt as if all the normal rules of life had been suspended. They spent the two days cheerfully labouring around the flood site, helping to clear the church and to shift people's possessions from Ful-End Cottages, they stayed up late, and they partook fully of the refreshments in the village hall where the W.I. had set up an on-going assembly line, providing tea, coffee, biscuits and sandwiches for all the workers.

Tom and Julie knew better than anyone how serious was the danger threatening the village, but of course they too were caught up in the excitement of the situation. Tom found his injured ankle frustrating, as it meant he couldn't help with the moving of furniture and other possessions. He would have loved to be one of those who loaded up barrows with people's stuff and swaggered up the street pushing them to safety, then returned again for more. This he had to leave to the more able-bodied folk, who included Julie, and Tony Foley. Meanwhile he made himself useful carrying messages and copying out lists of people's belongings so everything would eventually get back to where it had come from. Really, though, in the end he didn't feel too fed up about any of this; the important thing was that he was doing his bit towards the salvation of the village.

Everyone felt the same. People who had hardly ever spoken to one another in normal life became firm friends as they worked together towards this common goal. Tom realised to his surprise that he felt a lot less hostile towards Tony Foley. Somehow, they couldn't carry on being enemies when they were both busy helping his Nan move her stuff to a safe place. Nothing was as important as what they were doing together. It just wasn't possible to go on hating Tony when he sweated tirelessly up and down the stairs, red faced and hot, shifting the old lady's bits and pieces and calling their names out to Tom, who sat listing each item and where it belonged. The two boys exchanged grins and rolled their eyes at one another in sympathetic accord as she grumbled away.

"I'll never get me things straight again after all this. You wait, something's bound to get lost. Now you be careful of that picture, young Tony, it's worth a lot of money. Mind you, I won't have a wall to hang it on if there is a flood."

"Don't worry, Nan, you'll probably be back home with no damage done in a few days," Tony said reassuringly.

But this was the wrong thing to say too. Perversely, she now began to complain that nothing was going to happen.

"A lot of fuss for nothing, I shouldn't wonder. Could be tucked up in my own bed tonight instead of squashing in with you lot. Who says there's going to be a flood anyway?"

And as the hours went by and the weather didn't change much, it seemed as if the old lady was going to be proved right.

By Monday afternoon people weren't feeling so sure. A strong wind had blown up from the north-east, bringing with it some heavy bruise-coloured clouds and a few large drops of rain. By the time school finished the sky had a glowering look about it, the rain was now coming down much faster and trees were dancing dementedly in the wind. Cars had their headlights on, and shops and houses were lit up as if evening had already begun.

Tom looked anxiously down at the river. It was rushing along at high speed but had a long way to go before it reached danger level. Things still seemed as if they would be all right, Tom decided. He ambled on home, sucking a stick of raspberry toffee he had been given yesterday by Tony's Nan, who had a sharp tongue but a kind heart.

At tea, the talk was all about the weather. Everyone agreed that it was a nasty looking sky, but no one, not even Dad, who often tended to focus on the darker side of things, thought that there would be a flood.

"A lot of the snow's gone already," Gran observed. "It's been melting steadily for nearly a week now and no harm done."

"Could do without this downpour, though," Dad said as a particularly vicious squall rattled the windows and splattered a burst of rain onto the glass like a handful of gravel. "I'm not at all keen on you going out in it, Tom," he added. "What time's your rehearsal?"

"Half six. But I only have to go up to Adam's house for a lift. His Dad's taking a whole load of us to Fordinglye in his van, and he'll bring us back home too, so don't worry, Dad."

"Well, you be careful with that bad leg," said Mum "It's not the night for a lad in plaster to be out and about."

"Oh, Mum!" Tom had heard it all before. " 'Course I will."

He still felt light-hearted and optimistic as he set off a bit later, his recorder and music in the big inside pocket of his parka, to walk the fifty metres or so along the street to Adam's house. But as he battled through the gusty darkness some of this confidence started melting away. The weather really did seem to be getting worse all the time. He recalled that stormy night in December after he had first heard about the flood and the curse, and how frightened he had been when he thought he heard children sobbing over the sound of the wind.

Now he had arrived at today, the actual day when it seemed that the curse was due to be fulfilled, but instead of worrying about it, here he was heading cheerfully off to his rehearsal as if the danger was over. Had he gone mad! There would be children going out in the storm from all around the neighbourhood and beyond for this rehearsal; what unknown hazard might be in store for any of them?

Had he been distracted into a false sense of security by the weekend's hard work?

Just outside Adam's house he stopped, dithering between going in and trusting the plans made for lifts to the rehearsal at Fordinglye, or doing something else. Now that he was taking time to think about it, the doubts were queueing up inside his head waiting to be dealt with. How could he possibly have imagined that helping the grown-ups carry out flood prevention plans was enough to cancel out all the fears and warnings of the past few weeks?

Suppose, just suppose, that one or more of the children had for some reason or another failed to get the message about the rehearsal. They would be heading for Fulhurst Church instead of Fordinglye, heading perhaps for danger.

'But everyone for miles around must realise there might be a flood,' he argued with himself. 'No one would go down to the church in this, surely?'

Or would they? He thought of Mrs Hewittson, from the cottages. She'd not allowed any of her stuff to be moved and had absolutely refused to be persuaded to stay with friends in the village for the next few days.

"What nonsense!" she had exclaimed. "Never in all my life have so many grown people made such fools of themselves over nothing. Closing the church is downright wicked. If it isn't open as usual in the morning for early communion, I shall make a personal complaint to the bishop. Flood! Don't talk to me about floods!"

Were there others like Mrs Hewittson who had ignored the warnings? Or people who lived on the outskirts of the village or even farther afield, who didn't realise how serious things were? And if the message hadn't got through to their children, those children could be in Fulhurst Church even now, while the water in the river rose ever higher, and the Man in Black waited.

'I'll have to go and check the church,' Tom decided to himself, trying to be calm and practical. 'I can be there and back in twenty minutes. I'll just call at Adam's and say I've left something behind.'

"Hello Tom. Come on in out of the wet," Adam's mother held the door open for him, letting out an inviting golden shaft of light and warmth.

"Well, actually I just came to say sorry, but I've got to go home again first, I've forgotten something. But don't worry if I'm not back in time, Dad will take me if it gets too late." He was sure Dad would, although perhaps not very willingly.

"All right dear. They aren't ready to leave just yet, so with luck you should make it. Don't rush though, careful as you go — we'll wait for you as long as we can."

"Cheerio, Mrs Hayward. See you soon."

Trying to look casual and jaunty Tom turned away from the open door and limped back into the wind and the rain. He passed a couple of children on their way up to Adam's house, but further down, the street was empty. What a foul night it was! The rain flung itself in stinging gusts into his face, and the wind was so strong he was finding it hard to keep his balance; he didn't know whether the crutch made it easier or harder. As he approached the church a new sound added itself to those already in his ears — the roar of the river. Tom couldn't see very well but he could tell that it was a lot higher and wilder than it had been even a couple of hours ago when he set off home from school. He shivered. This was no place to be out and about in, on a stormy winter evening.

He turned towards the church. A quick look round would be enough, just to satisfy himself that there was no one there, then he could leave it to the night and the rain. It loomed in front of him, black and massive in the darkness. Tom's heart started to bounce uncomfortably as he tried to open the door. Suppose there was a great crowd of ghosts in there — the Man in Black and all the lost children?

Thank goodness, the cold metal ring in his hands wouldn't turn properly. The church was well and truly locked. With a sigh of relief Tom turned to retrace his steps back to the road, when with the side of his eye he saw something moving. There was a tall dark figure standing beside the vestry door, its long robe flapping in the wind.

"Oh no!" Tom whispered to himself in horror.

It must be the Man in Black. Who else could it be? But before Tom was really sure, the person moved out of the amber strip of light coming from the vestry door and was swallowed up by the darkness.

Why was the door open? And who could have turned the light on? Was there some perfectly normal explanation after all — Old Nick, for example, in his black winter overcoat, fetching his 'Noye's Fludde' score before going over to Fordinglye. Tom tried very hard to gulp down the lump of fear that had risen to the back of his throat, and called out.

"Hallo! Who's there?"

The door opened a little more, and a small face peered out.

"Is this the right place?" it asked anxiously.

Tom splashed over there as quickly as he could. The ground was very wet, squelching with his every footstep, and his crutch kept getting stuck in the mud. Surely there was even more water around than when he arrived a moment ago. Certainly, the patch of light from the open vestry door lay across a piece of ground shiny with water.

"Where's all the others?" asked the owner of the face by the door.

Tom could see now that it was a little girl, probably aged about six.

Behind her were five other children, all very small, none of them known to Tom.

"What happened? Where are you all from? Didn't you get the message?" Tom was through the doorway now, wet and blinking as his eyes got used to the light.

"We're from St Josephs. My mummy brought us all, but she had to leave us here early 'cos she needed to go to a meeting. She said all the others would be here soon. We didn't get no message."

St Josephs was a small Roman Catholic primary school on the south side of Lewes. Tom hadn't even known that the school was taking part in 'Noye's Fludde'.

"Why didn't you get the message?" he repeated, then, thinking of the figure he'd seen outside, he added "How did you get in?"

The little girl began to look distressed at this string of questions. She sniffed a couple of times before she was able to answer him.

"The Father let us in. Mummy said she couldn't wait but she's fetching us later after the rehearsal. I thought there was lots more coming."

"The Father? Whose father?" Tom began to feel a sick sensation at the pit of his stomach.

The poor little girl couldn't take any more questioning. The sniffing turned into tears. A boy, about the same age as her, took over.

"The Father, you know, the priest. He said he'd be back in a minute."

It all had an ominous sound to Tom. He must get them out of here fast. Trying to speak calmly so as not to upset any more of them he said, "Look, the rehearsal was changed 'cos there's flooding here. I don't know what happened to the message to your school, but never mind. I'll take you all to the vicarage and we can tell your mums and dads where you are. But we'd better be quick. It isn't safe here. WHAT'S THAT!"

They all heard it. It was a muffled, splintering sound from outside.

"Sounds like something fell over," said one little boy.

"Sounds as if the river's got through the flood barrier, more likely!" Tom responded grimly. This really was it.

"Look! There's water coming in!" the first little girl shrieked and pointed at the door. Where Tom stood, edging round his feet and the base of his crutch, was an advancing pool of water. Instinctively he lifted his injured leg away from it.

"We've got to get out of here. The river's flooding. We haven't much time." Tom's voice was urgent.

"I wanna go home. I want my Mum." The smallest boy's face crumpled suddenly, and he too began to cry.

Tom could see from their faces that the others were about to join in. As he frantically tried to think of some way of organising them there was another booming crash from outside.

"Quick, quick! We must get out now. It's no good climbing on the table, we'll all be drowned if we stay here. Don't cry. I know the way. But be quick. Hold hands, all of you, make a chain."

To the sobbing little girl he said, "You hold on to the back of my coat and follow me, everyone else hold on to the hand of the one in front of them. Keep moving."

They couldn't stop crying. The water was over their feet now, icy and heavy, dragging at their shoes and gumboots. But they did start moving, responding to the authority in Tom's voice and joining hands to follow him out of the church.

Outside, all around them the ground swirled and gleamed like black satin. Tom felt as if he had returned to the terrifying world of his nightmares. The roaring of the water, the sobbing of the children, the fear which was tightening in a suffocating band around his chest, all these were familiar from his dreams. But this was no dream, this was reality. He couldn't escape from it by waking up.

"It's in my boots. I can't walk, it's in my boots!" screamed the little girl who was holding onto Tom, jerking at him so he nearly lost his balance.

"You must walk." Tom turned and hauled her up, letting go of his crutch as he did so.

He didn't know if it was the numbing iciness of the water taking all feeling away from his feet, or the extreme urgency of the situation giving him the extra strength he needed, but he found he could manage without it. Perhaps it meant his ankle was nearly better. Anyway, it was taking his weight, and without the crutch he felt more in control.

Which way now? The river water would be all round the church and over the road as well, so there was no chance of getting to safety that way. The only way that might work would be to take them round the back of the church, through the churchyard and along the pathway which led up past the vicarage. Then they would be safe.

"Now, you must all hold on tight to each other. Never mind about shoes and feet getting wet. Just follow me!" He had to shout to make himself heard over the noise of the wind and the water.

The children were more or less silent now, some still sniffing and moaning a bit, but trying hard to do as he told then. He had to accept the fearful reality of the situation — that they were relying on him utterly, and that their lives were well and truly in his hands. The burden of responsibility he had been feeling over the past few weeks was nothing to this.

For the next few minutes, they all concentrated on wading through the deepening water, a bedraggled chain of small moving bodies. Above them the sky raged, hurling its wind and rain down with relentless violence. Around them the water pulled and surged, dragging at the children's shoes and boots which quickly became waterlogged and heavy.

Tom found it hard to hold on to his sense of direction. Surely they should have reached the churchyard by now.

"What's that! Oh, I don't like it," wailed someone as a row of ghostly grey shapes appeared in front of them like a set of silent sentinels.

Tom sighed with relief. "It's the churchyard," he panted. "Now, be extra careful here, because we'll sometimes be walking over the flat stones, and sometimes on the ground, so mind your feet."

"Oh no! Oh no! The bodies'll be floating about, there'll be all bones and skellingtons!" This howl was quickly echoed by several other children.

Tom realised that if he lost control now there would be no hope for any of them. He responded brusquely, pretending a confidence and strength he did not feel.

"Don't be silly. All the bodies are buried miles down. Come on, we're nearly there."

They would soon be at the gate to the vicarage garden. Yes, this must be it, sticking up pale and straight out of the water. But where were the lighted windows of the

156

vicarage, signals of their salvation? Why was it all dark? Suddenly an awful realisation hit Tom. Of course — the vicarage was locked up and empty! There would be no one living there until the new vicar and his family moved in next month.

Was it worth going on? He didn't think he had the strength to seek out the footpath from the end of the garden which Michael used to walk along on his way to and from school. So weary and chilled was Tom by now that all he wanted to do was to rest for a bit, to slip into the water and let the darkness take over. His leg throbbed too; it felt so huge and heavy that it seemed to be dragging him down, down below the water.

"Don't give up now. You'll all drown if you don't keep going."

Who was talking to him? Tom lifted his head and shook it to clear it of the mists which were swirling round inside it. Andrew Peck stood beside him. He smiled encouragingly at Tom.

"I'll stay with you and show you the way. Follow me."

So Tom did, leading his little band of children through the garden and up the track to the hill beyond, away from the water and the danger. No one else seemed to have noticed that Andrew was with them, but soon they all realised that they were walking, not wading.

"We're out of the flood!"

"Where are we going?"

"Just follow me."

Tom didn't really know the way in the darkness, but he was walking beside someone who did.

With the escape from immediate terror came enough confidence for the children to start crying again.

"I want my mummy."

"When are we going home?"

"I'm so cold."

"Why don't you get them to sing," Andrew suggested. "If they sing, they'll be able to keep going, and you too. And no one can sing and cry at the same time."

Tom remembered that he had his recorder, ready for that rehearsal which now seemed like part of another life, in the deep inside pocket of his parka. He pulled it out and shook it.

"Come on, kids, let's sing something to keep ourselves going."

Putting the recorder to his lips he lurched on, playing the first tune that came into his head — the animals' alleluia from 'Noye's Fludde'. Thin and ragged, quavering and uncertain, the voices of the children joined in. They all knew the tune; they were going to be playing some of the smallest animals in the performance.

So intent was Tom on playing his recorder, keeping his freezing fingers working over the holes and willing his legs to obey the pulse of the music, that he hardly noticed when Andrew turned to slip away.

"Goodbye, Tom, I must leave you here. But carry straight on, and soon you'll all be safe."

He had seen them safely past the hazard which had defeated him all those decades ago, the pond, treacherous and invisible in the darkness. Now he had completed what he had set out to do on that cold January day in 1837. He could rest in peace at last.

Tom and his followers went on, as if in a dream, the flimsy sound of their song blowing away in the squally air. Sometimes it seemed to Tom that there were not six, but more than a dozen children struggling along behind him, all the children who had ever been led away by the Man in Black. Had there ever been such a strange sight on the downs behind Fulhurst village as that forlorn little procession, all soaking wet and chilled to the bone, piping their tune in shrill little voices as they staggered, on the verge of total collapse, up the hill towards the ruins of Fulhurst Abbey?

Certainly it seemed not to Mr Nicholls, who was waiting for them under the shelter of the Abbey walls. He walked forward as they approached, a dark figure silhouetted against the beam of his torch, which he had balanced behind him on one of the empty window sockets.

Tom, looking towards the light, saw that tall black shape rise up and start moving towards them. It must be the Man in Black, come to claim the children.

"No, no! You can't have them!" he screamed, then collapsed onto the ground.

CHAPTER 18

Closure: The End of the Curse

"So it was thanks to Julie that we were there waiting by the Abbey," Mr Nicholls said. He was sitting with Tom and Julie in the lounge, visiting them at home just over a week after that fearful night, bringing with him a pile of newspapers, a sheaf of get-well cards made by Tom's schoolmates, and a large bunch of flowers.

Tom, looking pale and with a new plaster on his leg, was lying on the sofa, propped up with cushions. Several days had gone by since that nightmarish trek through the storm. All the little children were now fully recovered, but Tom himself had taken much longer to get over the ordeal.

He had been transferred straight to hospital that night, suffering from shock and exposure, and had spent the next couple of days in intensive care. Then as soon as he felt a bit better he had been wheeled off to the plaster theatre to have his ankle re-set. The healing bones hadn't broken again but they had become badly dislocated during the agonising trudge through the flood.

Now he was home again, and at last feeling a bit more like his old self, that self he seemed to have left behind for so long after the drama and tribulations of the past few weeks.

"Yes, you see," Julie took up the story. "They noticed pretty quickly you weren't there, at the Fordinglye Church, so after a bit Mr Nicholls went to the phone box and rang home to see where you were. Adam had told him you'd be coming with Dad. But of course, Dad didn't know anything about it. And then I suddenly thought that you might have gone down to check our church, so I got Dad to ask if anyone else was also missing. When we heard that the St Joseph's kids hadn't arrived either I was really worried…"

Mr Nicholls took over again.

"Of course, we'd already realised that the St Joseph's children hadn't come, but we just thought their parents had decided not to bring them out on such a filthy night, they were, after all, some of the very youngest of all those playing the animals and Fordinglye is further from Lewes than Fulhurst. Then Julie arrived with your father, having first persuaded him to go down to our church with her in case anyone was there. At that point I started to feel extremely concerned, because she took me aside and told me something of what the two of you had been up to in the last few weeks. She convinced me that you would have felt you needed to check the church, and that if you found anyone there you would head off uphill with them in the direction of the Abbey."

"So, you — well, you didn't think it was all a load of rubbish, sir? I mean, how much did she tell you about it all?" Tom felt rather shy asking this question. Could Julie have possibly dared to tell the whole extraordinary story to Old Nick, of all people?

"She didn't tell me everything then, but I think I know most of it now, and a very strange, sad story it is too. You poor chap, you have had a rotten time."

Sympathy, for some reason, made Tom's eyes prick and brought a lump to his throat. He gulped and blinked and managed to get his face back to normal, then turned the conversation again to the night of the flood.

"So what happened then?" he asked. "How come you were at the Abbey when we got there?"

"Well, by the time we arrived back in Fulhurst again there was no getting near the church; it was already more than knee-deep in water. Your father and quite a few others got together to go and look for you all — around the village and between here and Fordinglye, checking houses and so on. But Julie kept on insisting that you wouldn't have gone anywhere in the village, but that you would be making for the Abbey." He paused, glancing over at Julie with a slight smile, then went on:

"Not many people would listen to her, it seemed a crazy suggestion on such a night, but luckily, I did, and I said I would take her up there. You see, I do know something of the story of poor Brother Nicodemus. I suggested to those searching locally that if they hadn't found anyone and if we hadn't yet returned to the village, they should then make their way up to the Abbey to find us, and hopefully, to help bring the children down — which of course was what did happen. The quickest way to get to the Abbey was to drive back along the Fordinglye road, then to park the car and walk up the track behind the old Manor House. That was how Julie and I got there before you — and I gave you the fright of your life. I'm so sorry about that."

Tom shuddered, remembering their arrival and the figure of Old Nick, and thinking he was the Man in Black.

"If it hadn't been for Julie, goodness knows what would have happened." Mr Nicholls continued, "She was absolutely insistent, she said she'd go up there on her own if no one would take her."

"Thanks so much Jules; you've been absolutely amazing. I couldn't've done any of it without your help!"

Tom wasn't just thanking his sister for her part in the rescue, but also for her support and understanding throughout the whole business. On his own, he was sure he wouldn't have had the strength of mind to see the thing through. He had nearly given up so many times in the last few weeks.

"I'm just so relieved that you did all get there," Julie said with a slight shiver. She too would never forget that night, and the anxious wait with Mr Nicholls at the ruined Abbey.

"Still two things I don't understand, though," she went on. "One is why didn't St Joseph's get the message?"

"Ah, well," said Mr Nicholls. "That was due to one of those unforeseen events which no one could have anticipated. Obviously, we'd phoned round all the schools which had children taking part in the show, to tell them about the change of venue. In some cases, we had to leave messages if the school secretary wasn't able to come to the phone, which was what happened at St Joseph's. We actually left a repeat message a bit later as well. But late that morning there was a massive power-cut in a large area south of Lewes, caused I suppose by the oncoming stormy weather, which meant all the electricity went off. The school had to close and send all the children back home early because there was no power, no lighting or heating, so they never heard either message."

As Mr Nicholls finished his explanation a wonderful realisation spread through Tom. This time it really was all over. The fears and the anguish of the past few weeks were done with. With Julie's help and the kindly intervention of Andrew, the boy from the past, he had managed to do what he needed to do. Everyone was safe.

"That was what happened, wasn't it, Tom?"

Tom had missed Julie's second query. He focused again on what they were saying.

"What?"

"I was telling Mr Nicholls about the bloke you saw by the vestry door that night. The one those kids called 'The Father' and who you thought was the Man in Black — Brother Nicodemus — didn't you, Tom? But if he was a ghost, how could he open the door and turn the lights on? That's what I want to know."

Mr Nicholls had a possible explanation.

"Well, it's quite likely that it could have been the sexton. It's part of his job to lock and unlock the church, he's in charge of caring for the fabric and making sure everything is in order. He tends to wear a black cassock when he's on duty. Perhaps he opened the church earlier for that mother who'd brought the kids over, and also turned the lights on, intending to come back later to lock up — but of course by then it would have been too late because the church would have been flooded."

This was quite a plausible suggestion, which might have satisfied Julie, but Tom wasn't at all convinced. He knew the sexton, a short, plump elderly man, the absolute opposite of that tall, gaunt figure he thought he had glimpsed before he entered the church. He was sure it had been the Man in Black, coming to take the children away.

Mr Nicholls then glanced slightly anxiously at Tom, who, he now realised, had been coping with an overload of fear and stress for several weeks, and still looked fragile. He was as concerned about Tom's state of mind as his physical condition after everything he had endured, culminating in that shockingly perilous ordeal of rescuing the children. He continued carefully, trying to be both rational and calming.

"We could try to find out more, but would that be a good idea at the moment? Lots of strange things have happened, lots of things we can't explain. I think Tom

165

would do better for the time being at least to try and put that terrible night behind him as much as he possibly can and concentrate on getting well again. Thanks to the bravery of the pair of you, in the end there were no casualties, and everyone is safe. That's a triumph — and something to celebrate! Don't you think so, Tom?"

Tom nodded vigorously. There was nothing he wanted more than to get back to his old life.

"Oh yes, sir, I still can't believe that it really is all over — it's been going on for such a long time! Now p'raps I can think about normal things again! There's lots of stuff I still want to know. What happened about the rehearsal that night? What about 'Noye's Fludde'. Are we still doing it, sir?"

"Yes indeed," Mr Nicholls nodded, smiling again. "Don't worry Tom, it's all still going ahead as planned."

He began to explain about future rehearsals when there was a diversion. The door opened and in came Mum, carrying a tray of tea, cake and biscuits, with a bulky package tucked under one arm. Mr Nicholls stood up to take the tray from her.

"Look what has just arrived for you, Tom, love," she said, handing over the package.

It was a large parcel. Eagerly Tom ripped off the wrapping paper. It contained a big box of very expensive looking chocolates, and an envelope with his name on the front. Inside there was a card and a message.

'Dear Tom', it read, 'Please will you accept this very small token of our undying gratitude and heartfelt thanks to you for saving the lives of our beloved children. We do hope that you are feeling better by now. You are a hero! With very best wishes from the parents of Kim, Joanna, Timothy, Patrick, Vicky and Marcus.'

On the other half of the card the children had all written, in large uneven letters, their own names and lots of kisses.

"The six children," said Tom. "Isn't it funny, we went all that way together and I never found out any of their names." He paused, then added with a change of tone, "Anyway, who wants a chocolate?"

Julie picked something up from the floor. "Wait a minute, look, Tom. It must've fallen out of the card."

It was a fifty-pound note. Tom could hardly believe it. Fifty pounds, out of the blue!

"Hey, man; wicked! Fifty quid, FIFTY QUID!" he exclaimed, delighted and amazed.

Mr Nicholls got up to go, putting his empty teacup back on the tray.

"Time I was on my way," he said. "But very, very well done to the pair of you, you really are both true heroes! And get better soon, Tom — we all miss you at school! Oh, and don't forget to look at the papers!"

They had forgotten about the papers. There was a whole pile of them. Julie picked one up. To their amazement, Tom's face stared out at them from the front page.

'**HERO TOM SAVES THE CHILDREN!**' shrieked the headline of the Brighton Evening Argos.

"Ten-year-old Tom Lulham," it continued, "a native of the village of Fulhurst, which is recovering from the worst floods in living memory, saved the lives of six small children on the night of the storm. In the pitch-black darkness he led them away from the church in Fulhurst, where flood water had already risen to a dangerously high level, and took them all up onto the high ground behind the village where they would be safe.

"It was an astoundingly brave thing to do," said Martin Delaney, father of one of the children. "We can never forget what we owe him."

The report continued: "Such a feat would have been difficult enough for an able-bodied child. It was made all the more remarkable by the fact that Tom is suffering from an injured ankle and his leg is in plaster."

"I don't know how he did it," his proud mother told our reporter. For a fuller report and more flood stories and photographs go to page 17.

The press report from Lewes was even more dramatic:

'**CHILD OF COURAGE IN CRITICAL CONDITION AFTER REMARKABLE RESCUE DURING FULHURST'S NIGHT OF TERROR'** was the headline.

The report continued in the same style.

'White faced Sara and Robert Lulham sat by their unconscious son Tom's bedside last night in the intensive care ward at Lewes Victoria Hospital and prayed that he would live. Tom is dangerously ill with hypothermia and severe shock after heroically rescuing a group of very young Lewes schoolchildren from the Fulhurst flood, braving the storm and leading them away in the darkness, out from the semi-submerged church and up the hill to safety.'

"What a load of rubbish," remarked Tom, a bit embarrassed.

It felt strange, reading those stories about himself — the Tom Lulham of the news articles seemed to be a completely different person. As for the bit about him nearly dying, it simply wasn't true. He had been conscious all the time except when he had fainted on arriving at the Abbey, and then later that night when he fell asleep. He'd certainly never felt as if he was going to die.

Then there was all that about heroism and courage. Well, it might look like that on the surface, but of course the newspapers didn't know the real story at all. Surely anyone in his position would have done the same. He'd had no choice, it was as if he had been selected, then programmed, like a robot, to act as he did.

"Anyone who'd had the things happening to them that I did would've had to do it — like poor Andrew. Only I was lucky enough to make it," he said, thinking back to the turbulence and terror of that night.

"But you *were* really brave, Tom," Julie said. She rather liked the image of her brother as a hero.

"Well, only 'cos I absolutely had to do it. But oh God, Jules, I was terrified. I've never been so scared in my life — it was even scarier in a way than when I first saw the Man in Black. And I couldn't've done it if you hadn't helped me beforehand, or without Andrew Peck actually

169

helping me when I didn't think I could go on. So, I think we should share the fifty quid, because it was you as much as me."

"Tom! Really? Thanks! Just a bit of it though, you must have the most."

"No, I think we should split it down the middle. After all, if you hadn't believed what I told you after I came back from Brighton, and then had all the ideas for finding out what it was all about, I bet I would've given up."

"But the whole thing is 'ifs', really, when you look back on it," Julie reflected. "If Mr Nicholls hadn't decided to do 'Noye's Fludde', if you hadn't gone tobogganing and met the Man in Black…"

"If Ian and Mike hadn't moved away so I had to do things on my own, if Gran hadn't given me the skates so I went out to practice with them, then saw the Man in Black again and broke my leg, and if I hadn't broken my leg I wouldn't have been so fed up at school that I bunked off to Brighton…"

"And if you hadn't told me about it all, if we hadn't found those books at the library, if Christina hadn't come to stay the night and we realised about the old calendar — and so on and so on. It's ever so weird, the whole thing. The more you think about it, the weirder it is."

"All those ghosts," mused Tom. "I feel better about Andrew Peck now because he helped me, and because of that I think he's also OK now. But even though he was so frightening, I can't help feeling terribly sorry for the Man in Black, Brother Nicodemus. It was such an awful, awful thing to happen. No wonder he couldn't rest."

"Perhaps we should do something, something at the Abbey maybe," Julie suggested. "You know, something with singing, in the summer when the weather's good. If we did a show up there with singing in it, he might be able to rest in peace at last too."

Tom sat up, his eyes bright with excitement.

"Julie! Brilliant idea! Why not 'Noye's Fludde'? We could still have it as part of the anniversary celebrations, and also to raise money to help with the flood damage. I'm sure Old Nick would agree. Then lots more people would come, and Brother Nicodemus would see that there was singing going on again in the Abbey."

So it was, that on a mild summer evening the following June the Fulhurst village production of 'Noye's Fludde' took place in the open air around and inside the ruins of the old Abbey. Tom, on both his legs again, was singing Jaffet. Tony hadn't minded because he had done it in the spring performances. They had become good friends, those two, to everyone's surprise including their own.

The performance was nearly over. Tom, raising his voice with the rest of the cast in the final hymn, wondered if that restless unhappy ghost which haunted these ruins was listening. Was it his imagination, or could he see a lonely black-clad figure standing quietly in one of the shadowed alcoves of the Great Church?

When it had ended, and the audience members were wandering down the hill, back towards the village, Tom lingered behind for a moment.

"Goodbye, Brother Nicodemus," he said softly, talking to the shadows. "We'll come back again every summer to sing in your Abbey, I promise."

"Tom! TOM! Oh, there you are!" Julie appeared outside one of the empty arches. "Come on! There's a giant tea party down in the village hall, and all the ice cream'll be gone if we don't hurry!"

"Coming!"

And Tom dashed joyfully away leaving his ghosts behind him for ever.

THE END